# Alexander

## THE JAMES CHILDREN SERIES BOOK 2

# KATHI S. BARTON

This is a work of fiction. Names, characters, places, and incidents are products of the author's imagination or are used fictitiously and are not to be construed as real. Any resemblance to actual events, locations, organizations, or person, living or dead, is entirely coincidental.

**World Castle Publishing**
Pensacola, Florida

Copyright © Kathi S. Barton 2012
ISBN: 9781938243240
First Edition World Castle Publishing May 5, 2012
http://www.worldcastlepublishing.com

**Licensing Notes**

Cover: Karen Fuller
Editor: Brieanna Robertson

# Chapter 1

"Just let me finish. I want you to listen to me then make your decision. Why do you have to be so stubborn? Damn it, man."

Alexander watched his friend and partner pace in front of him. This meeting with Brick Wells was long overdue. He knew that Brick was going to be pissed about this, but the way Alexander saw it, they were both going to be much happier.

"I want to take on this project. I know you have reservations about —"

"I don't have reservations," Alexander interrupted Brick. "I said I don't think the guy is trustworthy. If you want to go ahead with this then do it. I want no part of it."

Brick sat down hard in the chair. He looked at Alexander and he knew that he'd seen none of the terror he felt for him. There was something about this deal that Alexander thought was just a little too good to be true. And as he'd heard all his life, if it felt that way, then it more than likely was.

"Then I guess this is it. After all these years, you're leaving." Brick rested his head in his hands and looked at him through his fingers. "I never thought it would come to this. I thought for sure it would be over a woman."

Both men laughed. "I don't have time to date. Maybe if you give me the right price, I'll make the time."

They had been partners in A&B Computers since they'd met in college. Alexander had been a ripe old age of sixteen and Brick a year older. The two boys had hit it off immediately, saving one another from having the crap beat out of each other every other day instead of every day. Alexander grinned when Brick looked down at the new wedding ring on his finger.

"Amy is going to be pissed about this. She said I was to make you see it my way or I would end up alone in the office every night trying to do the work of both of us."

Alexander stood up and put his hand out to Brick. "Tell her that you had me nearly in tears and that I only caved when my mom called."

Brick took the offer of the hand. "You're going to regret this. You're going to be sitting in a posh restaurant and read how I am the richest man in the world because my ungrateful friend ran out on me when I was making it big."

"I hope so. I sincerely do." Alexander looked around his office. "I've been in this office more in the past ten years than I ever was in my house. I need this more than you know."

Brick left telling Alexander that he would contact his lawyer and have him draw up the papers. In just a few short weeks, Alexander was going to be a very wealthy unemployed computer programmer.

Alexander supposed if one had to spend a great deal of time in an office, this wasn't all bad. There was the view for one thing. He could see all of the wooded area behind their office building for miles. Then there was the office itself.

The desk was an antique walnut that his mom and he had refinished the year before he'd moved into this building with it. The chair was new, only about six months old, but it was comfortable and big, something a man his size needed to have when he spent a lot of time in it.

One whole wall was devoted to pictures. Alexander knew he had a good eye for a shot and prided himself on some of the covers he'd graced, such as *LIFE* and also a few outdoorsmen magazines.

He'd also done a great deal of traveling in his job. The second wall, covered in shelves, held treasures he'd brought, been given, and also had found. He had spent an entire summer on a dig a few years back and had been able to keep a couple of the things he'd unearthed. The last wall was an open, glassed wall that spilled into the offices beyond.

He could sit and watch all the hustle and bustle of all the employees they'd acquired over the years. Last count there had been seventy-three and growing. Well, growing for Brick. He turned back to his desk.

The picture of his sister and her husband Jared was to his left and the one of his parents to his right. He chuckled a little when he thought of Brick's desk and the multitude of pictures he had of his wife on every surface. When someone knocked at Alex's door, he looked up to see his secretary Deb Smith.

"Mr. James, is it true? You're leaving?" She didn't look overly upset. He knew that he'd been hard on her for the past several weeks, but it was because she was so damned annoying.

"Yes. I should be gone in about a month, if not sooner. I'm sure that Brick will find a place for you in the business." He hoped so, at least. Brick didn't care for her either. "There will be all sorts of jobs opening with the new contract."

"Nope, but thanks. I'm leaving too. I only stuck around to see if…well, it doesn't matter now anyway."

When she left, Alexander laid back and closed his eyes. He decided to call a travel agent and book a long vacation. But first, he was going to visit his parents.

They had just recently moved closer to Columbus. It was a four hour trip for him to go there, less if he didn't obey the speed limit. He was just getting ready to call them when his phone rang. He smiled when he saw who it was.

"I was just getting ready to call you. What are you and Mom doing this weekend?"

His dad laughed. "Calling to see what it would take to persuade you to come here. Willow and Jared are having an open house on Sunday, whatever the heck that is. Seems Jared is going to cook. Boy isn't half bad." Alexander heard mumbling in the back ground. "Damn it, Amanda, I was just kidding."

"Dad, what's going on? Is Mom giving you a hard time again?" Alex laughed again as the mumbling got heated. After several minutes of this, Alex spoke again. "Dad, talk to me or Mom."

"She wants to know if you're coming up. Said to tell you that you are long overdue for a hug." Edgar James, Alex and Willow's dad, was one in a million. "She wants you here. She misses you. She was talking about you over bridge the other day."

Alex burst out laughing. "Mom hasn't played bridge in her life. You'd better start taking notes, Dad, you're slipping. I'll be there. I have something I want to tell you all anyway."

"If you tell us you've met some girl you can't live without, I'll throw a party. Hell, son, I'll have three parties."

Alex sat back in his chair before he answered. "Wills is the one who's going to give you tons of grandkids. I'm happy just the way I am. No, I've not met a girl, nor do I ever have any intentions of meeting one." Alex had thought once was enough for any person. "I'll leave here after work. I'll stay at the hotel on Fifth if there's room."

"No, Wills and Jared said they have plenty of room. Your mom and I are actually going to stay too. The addition they put on is finished along with the pool. Might be nice to swim a bit without all those people around."

The James' owned hotels. Not just hotels, he supposed, but chains of the best in the world. The James family had been in the hotelier business for four generations and Wills would be the fifth when she was ready. Or he supposed when Dad was ready. They hung up a few minutes later. With nothing else to do, Alex packed up his laptop and left for his sister's house.

~~~

Jared walked up behind his wife and wrapped his arms around her waist. He rested his chin on her shoulder and waited. She had called him at the site today and asked him not to work late. He thought she was nervous about the two families coming to stay, but now he wasn't so sure.

"The Findley building will be finished two weeks early if we stay on schedule and under budget too." She was the best foreman their company had. "I had to fire Sloan Concrete today. The stuff they sent over again was shit."

He kissed her shoulder before commenting. "I guess the talk with the owner didn't do us any good."

They stood there at the French doors in their bedroom just looking out. The view was spectacular. They had added this suite of rooms when they'd remodeled, adding a library and office for them in addition to the bedroom they now shared. The bedroom they had started out in was now a guest room.

They stood there for a few minutes more before she spoke again. "I fell at work today."

Jared stiffened. When he started to turn her around, she wrapped her fingers around his wrist and held him still.

"Willow, what happened? Were you hurt?" He was afraid for her and about her. He couldn't think past her being hurt.

"Conley called an ambulance and then pissed me off because he made me go with them. He said he was going to call you if I didn't. I tried to tell them it was nothing."

Jared decided he was going to have a long talk with Conley next time he saw the man. "He should have called me anyway." He kissed her again. It was better than strangling her. "Did you threaten him again? Damn it, Willow, I'm your husband. I need to know when you're hurt."

She nodded. When she pulled away, he let her. Something more was going on. She sat on their bed and began to cry. Jared went to her immediately and pulled her into his arms.

"I'm pregnant. The doctor said I wasn't eating right nor was I rest—"

His mouth covered hers and silenced her. He lowered her to the mattress and rolled over to his back, bringing her with him. She lay over him and he opened his legs to cradle her closer.

"From now on," he began as she settled on his chest. "You'll eat breakfast *and* lunch. No more skipping meals. I'll bring you lunch and eat with you. That way I can...what?"

She was giggling. He thought it was better than tears, but he didn't like them any better. He pulled her closer, kissed her on the mouth, and swatted her ass too.

"Hey, mom-to-be here. What was that for anyway?" She shifted over him and stilled suddenly. "You're very hard, Mr. Stone. Do you want something?"

Her voice was husky and warm. He rocked upward and moaned when she pressed down onto him. He wondered if there was ever going to be a time when he didn't want her like he did now, like he did every time she touched him.

"Willow, you keep this up and your parents are going to wonder what's taking us so long." Until that second, he'd forgotten they were downstairs. "Unless of course you don't care. At this moment, I certainly don't."

He grunted when she rolled off him. Then he groaned and reached for her. Her nipples were poking through her shirt. His mouth watered to taste them. She stepped back when he reached for her.

"Please, baby. Just a taste. A little something to tide me—" He nearly swallowed his tongue when she lifted her shirt and bra up over her breasts.

The bounce is what had him whimpering. When her breasts bounced and quivered slightly, he reached down and rubbed his hand over his cock. Her nipples, always a source of delight for him, were hard and long. Sitting up on the bed then sliding to the floor, he crawled to her on his knees. He took one hard tip into his mouth and suckled. Hard.

"Jared, please. Please make me come. I need it so bad." Never one to deny her, he pulled the snap open on her jeans and yanked them down panties and all.

"Christ, you're wet," he moaned as he buried his fingers in her slit. "You're going to owe me for this, baby. I'm going to need you hard and dirty later."

"Yes. Please, just hurry."

He made his way down her torso, nipping and kissing her exposed skin as he went. When he got to her navel, he whirled is tongue deep as he continued to fuck her with his fingers. She rocked into his hand.

When he was near her apex, he looked up at her face. Lust, hunger, and desire were written there. She watched him as he kissed her trimmed nether lips.

"You'll have to be quiet when you come. If not, then everyone will hear you." She nodded. "Can you be quiet, baby?"

Jared's cock hurt. He wanted her, wanted to bury his cock deep into her pussy and never leave. He couldn't wait until later. He needed her now.

"Baby, I—"

She moved away and back then went to the edge of the bed. Bending over at the waist, she spread her legs wide and then looked back at him. Standing quickly, Jared opened his fly and freed his cock quickly. It was already dripping with his need.

Not saying a word, he walked up behind her and entered. She tightened around him immediately, her sheath rippling along his cock and milking him. He knew she was coming and could barely hear her screams as she buried her face in the blankets.

Moving out to the tip of his cock, he slammed hard back into her. His fingers dug deep into her flesh at her hips. He held her still while he fucked her. He could feel his balls tighten up and fill. Three then four strokes and he felt his own release hammer at him. It was all he could do not to roar out her name as she came again.

# Chapter 2

Alex left his apartment later than he'd wanted. So now it was nearly seven in the morning and he was starving. He knew he'd be welcomed at either house, his sister's or his parents', but he wanted to just have a few minutes of quiet time and some strong coffee.

He was driving down the main street — he thought it was actually called Maple Avenue — when he saw the little shop. They were doing a good bit of business, he saw, and after finding a parking place nearly a block away, he went inside House of Aromas.

Alex was nearly bowled over by two women in business suits with two white and pink striped boxes tied with strings in their hands. Each of them smiled up at him as they clutched their boxes and hurried out the door. When Alex turned back, he felt his belly rumble and his nose flare.

The shop was named well, he decided. The smells emanating around the room were strong and delicious. Blueberries and cinnamon, apples and chocolate just to name a few of the warm scents that made his mouth water for a taste. He looked around the small shop as he made his way to the front counter.

There were about a dozen or so tables, some with two chairs and others with four. All of them were striped with the pink and white material. And all of them were occupied.

The walls were a bright white and one of them was covered with framed pictures. Even from halfway across the room, he could see that the majority of them were of people and nearly all of those had some sort of dessert in them. There were even a few wedding cakes with brides and grooms.

The opposite wall was a mural of the area right around the shop, including the shop itself. Alex guessed the early fifties if the cars were any indication. The shop was in the middle of the painting with a woman and three young boys out front. It didn't look the same as it did now.

The building then had been a one-story with an awning out front. It was a brighter pink than was being used now, but with the name of the shop in a very nice script. No stripes, though. The building now was a nice two-story with two large display windows out front filled with antiques from the time period and baking pans. The awning was still pink and, of course, now striped.

But it was the counter that has his full attention now. Alex would bet that it was one of the original display cases on the left with the one on the right being new and much bigger. The lighting and glass shelves were in the new, as the older one had a wooden shelf filled with beautiful displays. He wondered how they could get away with that and the board of health when he saw that pastry items in this one were plastic. And very good models at that. He grinned at the woman behind the counter when she spoke to him.

"What'll you have?"

She looked happy, Alex realized with a start. He was so used to seeing the wait staff at the coffee shop he went to looking surly and bored that he was caught momentarily speechless. When she blew a wisp of hair out of her eyes and winked, he laughed.

"I'm sorry. Owner?"

She shook her head at his question. "Nah, Mom's in the back. She's trying to talk the delivery guy out of holding her flour hostage for a date. Guy never gives up. You need her?"

"I was just going to tell her what a charming place she has here. Will she be long, you think?" He didn't know why, but he really needed to tell her. "I can come back if she's really busy."

She opened the gated counter and let him through, but not before saying he should try and make the guy see reason. Alex wanted to help, but decided he shouldn't get involved. If she needed help with the guy, he would only do so if she asked him to.

"I'll see what I can do for her." She mumbled her thanks and shouted for the next person to order.

He wasn't sure what he'd expected, but it wasn't even close to what he walked into. The big, burly guy had an older woman pressed against the wall and was groping her. She was beating him against his shoulders and even with the man's hand over her mouth, he could hear her screaming. Tears streamed down her face.

Without thinking about what he was doing, he walked across the room and jerked the guy away. As the woman crumpled to the floor, Alex went after the man.

"She wanted it. You can't blame a guy for—" he started.

"Sure I can," Alex snarled at him. "And I'm going to enjoy showing you how it feels to have your rights taken from you."

The first punch caught the man in the nose. Blood gushed forward even as the man staggered away. The second caught him in the jaw and had him hit the wall behind him. Alex wasn't sure how much longer he might have enjoyed using the man as a punching bag, but he slid to the floor unconscious. Alex took several deep breaths before he turned to the woman.

She grinned up at him, her lip swollen and bleeding. "You're not supposed to be back here. But I've never been so happy to see anyone in my entire life."

He helped her to a chair and when he got her seated, he handed her a towel that was nearby. She put it to her mouth and looked up at him. "Thanks," she said.

"My pleasure. I think you should call the police now. He assaulted you." Alex looked around the room for a glass to give her a drink as he continued. "The girl up front, she told me I could come back and tell you what a great shop you have."

"Yeah, real nice. I'm not sure...he never..." She shuddered. "He's a bastard and I hope to hell he loses his job."

Alex couldn't help it; he threw back his head and laughed. "So do I. And if he doesn't, we'll have to make sure he does in another way."

~~~

Heather Laird stacked the plates on the tray and picked up the heavy burden. Four more hours. Four more hours and she could go home and see the love of her life,

Jack. Well, she amended, one of the loves of her life. Big Tom, her grandda, would be there too.

Heather dumped the glasses and threw out the trash as she stacked all the dishes she'd just bussed off her table with a practiced ease. When the dishwasher guy, Mike, came back, he grinned at her.

"Ain't nobody helps me out but you, Heather." He began loading the dirty dishes onto the rack. "'Course none of them others is as sweet on me as you are either." He winked at her when she laughed.

"That's right. When are you going to marry me and take me away from all this, Mike?" It was an old joke between the two of them.

He stacked the last dish, opened the door to the ancient dishwasher, and slid the rack inside. When the door was closed again, he hit the switch that started the washer and started loading the next rack as he answered her. "Well for one, I'm old enough to be...we're gonna say daddy but we both know I'm closer to be your granddaddy. Second, and more importantly, my wife would skin me alive. That woman is the sweetest person I know next to you, but damned if she don't scare me to death at times." He winked again. "Besides, you need to find you a nice young buck to take you places. You work too hard."

Heather looked away. It was always like this when someone mentioned her getting married or dating. She'd get scared then teary. When she was exhausted like she was now, it wasn't always easy to put up a front. But she knew Mike wouldn't comment on the tears or pry so she let a few of them fall. She hated self-pity, but also knew she didn't fall this far into a pity party often.

When Charlie the cook yelled her name, she took the paper towel Mike shoved at her and went to get her order. She glanced at her watch. Three and a half hours to go.

She'd been waiting tables since she'd been fifteen and on her own. It wasn't until later, after her grandda had found her living in the shelter, that she'd found the two of them an apartment. Then when she'd had Jack, Grandda had stayed. Thomas Laird couldn't have come at a better time. She had sobbed when he had told her he was staying to help, telling her that he would have talked to his daughter, Heather's mom, if she wanted. She didn't, and only when her mother called did the man speak to his daughter.

He told her he hadn't known about what had happened to her. Her mother had thrown her out the day she'd found out she was pregnant. She'd never asked about the boy...man really, but had blamed her for her stupidity and told her when she gave the baby up or got rid of it any other way, she could come home. Heather hadn't spoken to her since. And Jack, her son, was still hers.

At ten minutes until six, her last table had been bussed and she had already filled the sugar containers and salt and pepper shakers. Her replacement, Bailey, was there on time for a change. Heather was on her way home at five after and was smiling for the first time all night.

Grandda and Jack were having a heated debate over football again. Jack was a diehard Bengals fan and her grandda the Browns. Heather smiled as she put her coat in the closet. It seemed both teams had lost. Again.

"I did not say they were hopeless, young man. I said the situation was. They have no defense and as far as—"

"Have you been watching your own team, Grandpa Tom? They suck." She walked into the kitchen in time to see Jack put his plate on the counter instead of the sink. "The only reason they know what game they're playing is because the ref hands them the ball every time."

"Why you little turd. If you were my kid, I'd wash your mouth out with soap." Grandda stood and moved toward Jack. "I just realized you are mine."

They both dissolved into laughter as she stepped further into the room. "Has another crises been averted or do I need to go out and come back in for round two?"

Jack untangled himself first from the spry sixty-eight-year-old still on the floor. He got up slower than his great grandson, but no less happy to see her, she could see.

"We were debating on the super bowl chances of our teams. Your son has a smart mouth. I wonder where he gets that from," he asked her as he kissed her cheek.

Heather only smiled. His mouth could be just as sassy as hers was and he knew it. She went over to the counter and looked down at Jack's empty plate. Without a word, he picked it up and rinsed it off before putting it in the sink along with his empty glass and silverware.

While Jack went to gather his book bag, she tidied up the rest of the kitchen. She knew it had been Jack's turn to cook because the kitchen was only slightly out of order. Grandda would have made a mess like he was cooking for three times what they had to eat. She turned to look at him when he coughed again.

"Spill it, old man. I'm too tired to try a guessing game. Besides, you look like you're about to burst open." When he gestured toward a chair, she froze inside. "What's happened? Tell me."

"Your mom called again. Now don't go off pissy," he said when she rose up to leave. "She asked after the boy. Then she said…she wanted to know if you'd come to your senses yet."

She looked at him, confused. Then it hit her. "She still thinks I should give him up. After all this…doesn't she realize that he's mine? That I love him more than my own life?"

Her grandda snorted. "She no doubt gets it now. Had a few words with her myself. Can't believe I had such a selfish bitch for a child."

Heather laughed. Her mother was in her early fifties and far from being a child. But she wisely kept her mouth shut. She looked at her grandda and kissed him.

"I'm sorry, Grandda. I'm so sorry you had to lose a daughter over this. I love you very much."

"I wouldn't have it any other way honey." He got up to pace. "She said I was an old fool for helping you out. Said I was being bilked. Bilked outta what, I asked her. Here we are living off you working three jobs and my social security and don't have two cents to rub together. You know what I told her? That I ain't been happier in my whole life since my Colleen died. Why, Jack and you make me young."

Heather got up and hugged her grandda. "I love you so very much." He blushed bright red and gathered his things for his job.

He was a greeter for Wal-Mart three days a week. He said he did it for the money, but she thought he'd gotten himself a girlfriend. She hugged him again as he went out the door. The rest of the morning was spent on giving Jack a once-over of his spelling words and him helping her with her homework. He handed her the permission slip reluctantly. He and his class were to go to COSI, the Center of Science and Industry, the following week and the children were required to bring a minimum of twenty dollars to pay for bussing and their lunch.

"I don't care if I go, Mom. The teacher said that some of the kids who didn't want to go could spend the day in the library reading. I really like to read, you know." She looked at her son and wondered not for the first time when he'd gone from the baby she'd brought home to the grown child in front of her.

"Jack, we always have the money for your school." She got up from the table and began cleaning the already spotless counter. "I'm sorry, little man. Sorry every day I can't give you more. But I just couldn't let you go after I saw you."

He didn't say anything, but she heard him move his chair. When his arms wrapped around her from behind, she felt tears spill over her cheeks.

"Is this 'cause of Vickie?" Jack had never called her mom anything but by her first name. Heather nodded. "Poop on her. I heard Grandpa Tom yelling at her. He sure was mad."

"He told me. He said she was selfish." Heather had a moment to wonder if there had been more than grandda had told her. When Jack spoke, she knew there had been.

"He sure can string together some cuss words when he wants, huh? I would have gotten my butt blistered but good if I'd said only one or two of them." She knew he was laughing; she could feel him shaking behind her.

She turned around and looked down at him, fighting her own laughter. "See that you don't. You'll never be too big for me to spank."

He was out the door ten minutes later to catch the bus. Heather sat down heavily in the chair and looked around their home. They'd lived here for eight years and it looked it. The counters were a worn yellow with a few patches of white. The appliances were old and the stove worked when it suited. The ice machine had never produced a single cube since they'd moved in.

The floors were clean, she saw to that, but worn in so many places it resembled a patch work quilt rather than a floor. She'd made curtains once, but they'd long since been thrown out. The table and chairs, along with the rest of the furniture throughout the apartment, was third if not fourth hand. The plates were mismatched, as were the glasses and silverware. The place was a dump, a clean dump, but a dump nonetheless. But it was cheap, something that they needed as much now as they had then.

As she made her way to her room to take a nap before her next job, she locked up and turned off lights and wondered if things could get any worse.

# Chapter 3

Alex hugged his sister to him again. He was still trying to wrap his mind around the fact that she was married and now she was pregnant. And even though he and Jared were friends, he was still trying to figure out if he was pissed off at him or not.

"Stop glaring at him," Wills said as she punched him. "We didn't do anything you haven't done a thousand times before."

"I'll have you know that I never got anyone's sister pregnant. That I know of. And I thank you for the high opinion you have of my sex life." He kissed her again. "But a big brother is entitled to be a little thrown when he finds out his baby sister is knocked up."

"Such language," Amanda admonished him as she came into the room. "Women aren't knocked up when they are married, they glow."

Alex smiled at his mom as she sat next to Jared. He stuck his tongue out at Alex. He glared; Wills laughed at her husband. They all looked at his mom when she simply cleared her throat.

"So," Edgar James said as he came into the room. "Tell us more about what happened at the bakery. By the way, House of Aromas is now my favorite new place. These muffins are the best."

Alex had brought them a dozen of the muffins from the shop. Caroline Shafer, the woman he'd saved from certain rape, had been so grateful she'd told him he had whatever he wanted for life. He assured her that he wouldn't live long with an offer like that, but he would come by once in a while for some muffins.

"The police were very nice. They told Caroline that he'd probably done it before and gotten away with it. She said he was the best wholesale distributor as far as pricing goes around the state." Marta, Jared and Wills' housekeeper, came in with fresh coffee as he continued. "She said he'd been asking her out, but she'd said no every time before, including today. She said she couldn't figure out what he would want from a woman three times his age."

"Could be he's a mite on the sick side," Marta said as she sat down. "I know Miss Caroline. She's a friend of my mamma's. Her mamma used to bake all the pastries that come outta that shop afore she passed on. Hear tell Miss Caroline got her a good cook in Missy Laird. You met her, Master Alex?"

"No. Just the daughter, Lisa. She seems like a nice girl." When they all turned to look at him, he stood and stretched. "I'm going to bed before you all have me married off to the baker's daughter." He went up to the room his sister had taken him to when he'd arrived. He was smiling when he entered, thinking about their faces when he'd told him he was selling out to Brick in a few weeks.

His dad had been the first to recover. Grabbing him in a bear hug, he'd told him now he, too, could move closer. His parents had sold their house in Virginia not long after Jared and Wills had returned from their honeymoon. Alex thought that Jared's parents had done the same thing and had moved close enough to be considered neighbors.

The room he was in was huge, bigger, he thought, than his entire apartment back in Cincinnati—and much homier. The bed was a monster of a four poster that fit his six-foot-six frame easily. The furniture, all antiques, was dark cherry and polished to a bright sheen. Lying down on the bed, he thought about the shower he'd used too.

Six sprays, three on both sides of him, and the large overhead spray as well. The water had tumbled down over his head like a gentle rain, warm and soft. He didn't think he'd ever enjoyed anything so much as that in a very long time. He rolled over to his back and wondered if he needed to start dating more if a shower was the best thing he'd experienced in some time. He was drifting off when he realized he should sell his stuff and move up here.

~~~

Heather was pulling out her first batch of cookies as Caroline told her about the delivery guy. Heather wasn't sure who the guy was as she'd never met the people who came in before she did, but she heard about him often enough.

"Are you all right then?" She looked over her boss and thought she looked better than she had in a while. "I hope you called the police."

"Yes. Yes. They came and took him away in the ambulance. I had a hero. Something James, I don't remember his first name. He came right back here and knocked the kid on his ass." Caroline laughed as she told the story.

Heather had worked for "House" six days a week baking and decorating whatever Caroline needed. Sometimes more when she needed her to do a wedding cake or some other special project. Caroline had agreed to work around her schedule of needing to be off by three in the afternoon and had only had to miss that time once in all this time. At one o'clock, Heather was pulling out the last cake she'd decorate tomorrow when she came in and only had another two batches of cookies to bake. The loaves of bread just needed to cool enough to put into the wrappers and then she was finished. When the phone rang up front, Lisa yelled back to get it, please. Heather picked up the extension and a pen.

"Caroline, please?" The voice was very male and one Heather didn't recognize.

"She's not here right now. I don't know when she'll be back. Can I take a message for you?" Heather pulled the pad closer to write whatever order the guy wanted, hoping she had it already finished.

"She asked me to call her at this time. Tell her it's James and she'll come to the phone. It's all right, kid. Just do it."

Heather didn't like being talked to as if she were stupid. The man's tone made her think he was a guy used to getting what he wanted when he wanted it. "I'm not in the habit of lying, sir. But I will give you the benefit of the doubt because you don't know me. But I assure you, she's not here. If you want me to take a message for you, then I will."

"I never said you were...damn it. I refuse to explain myself to you. Put her on the fucking phone like a good girl and I won't get you into trouble." His voice had taken on a very forceful tone now. She didn't like it any better than she did being called a liar — twice now.

"You're so right. You don't have to explain your high and snotty self to me. Goodbye." She wanted to slam the phone down and hurt his ears, but she gently returned it to the cradle.

When it rang less than a minute later, she picked it up before Lisa did. She knew it was him, at least she hoped so. She smiled when he started sputtering.

"You hang up on me again and I'll have your ass fired. Put Caroline on the fucking phone right now." He was snarling now and for reasons she couldn't explain, that made her laugh out loud. "You won't think it's so funny when I get there."

Heather was still laughing as she finished up the bread and cookies and put on her coat. After telling Lisa she'd be back later tonight, she slipped out the back door just as she heard the bell in the front part of the building ringing. She walked the seven blocks to her next job with a small skip in her step.

Her pants she'd worn to the bakery were fine. She pulled the half shirt on that was her uniform at the bar. She hated it, but the tips were good and she needed the extra money the patrons tipped her because she wore it.

She did notice that she had to cinch up her belt another notch. She tried to remember if she had actually eaten lunch today or had she only thought she had? Grandda was going to be upset with her if he noticed she'd lost more weight and decided to make sure her shirts were a little baggy until she had time to put a little weight back on.

Heather was beat. She didn't know how much longer she was going to be able to keep going on the little cat-naps she was getting every day. Pulling out the picture of Jack and Grandda she'd taken a few weeks ago, she sat down and closed her eyes. For them, she'd do about anything.

She opened her bag and took out her book and lessons. One more class, six more weeks, and she'd have her high school diploma. She was twenty-six years old and was finally going to get it. She brushed angrily at her tears. At least she was trying. But she knew it was more for Jack than anything. He was her own personal cheering squad and every time one of her papers came back with an A on it, he'd hang it on the refrigerator next to his.

She supposed she could have gotten her GED by now. It was only a test and she could have had this done. But she wanted to have a real education, with lesson plans and homework. It had taken her three years of working when she could, making payments she could ill afford, but it was going to be worth it. She could go to college and make something of herself when she was finished.

"You ever come up for air?"

Heather looked up, startled.

"I said you ever come up for air. You been at it for over an hour." Bob pointed to the book in front of her.

"I was just reading. Do you need something?" She closed her book, embarrassed to be caught studying. No one knew her situation. None of the places knew all that much about her and she liked it that way. No one knew about her lack of education and absolutely no one knew about Jack. She'd made that mistake before and had nearly lost Jack over it. They all knew she had other jobs, but not where or that she was barely scraping by.

"Wondered if you'd like a bowl of soup? I need someone to tell me if it's okay for the Friday night gang." He set down a huge bowl and spoon in front of her. "I call it 'Bob's Dumps.' Made the dumplings myself."

She picked up the spoon after stashing away her book. The soup smelled wonderful and looked good too. She cut a dumpling in half with a great deal of effort and put it into her mouth. She should have known that it would be tough. What she didn't know is that it'd be crunchy.

She couldn't stop the grimace that she knew he'd seen. She chewed harder and decided that she'd break a tooth before she spit it out. When she finally managed to swallow, she looked up at him. She wasn't sure how to tell him.

"That bad, huh?" He took the spoon out of her hand and took both the bowl and it to the sink. "Can't seem to make them fluffy like the book says."

"I can do it for you." The words were out of her mouth before she thought. "I'm sorry, Bob. That wasn't very nice. I'm sure they'll love them."

He turned and looked at her with a complete look of horror on his face. "They'll cut my nuts off and serve them to me if I serve them this swill. Lucky thing I only cooked this one. This way I can salvage the...the soup part was okay, right?" he asked suddenly.

"Yes. That was...Mr. Bob, if you want me to, I can...I can make dumplings for you."

He walked over to the stove and began fishing out the rest of the dumpling he'd made. Without turning from the pot, he spoke to her. "If you can do it, please do. They wanted dumplings so I gotta have them. Come on, sweetie, help an old man out."

She stood up and moved to his work counter. In less than twenty minutes, she had a batch of her dumplings whipped up, and while he divided up the soup into four pots, she measured out enough batter for five more batches.

"You can only cook a few at a time or they won't be right," she told him as she dropped them by tablespoons full into the bubbly liquid. "If you do it this way, you can drop more into the broth while you serve up the other pots."

For another half an hour, she simmered dumplings and made three more batches of them up for him. By the time she was ready to start tending bar, Bob had enough fluffy dumplings to feed an army, or thirty men watching football on the big screen.

By midnight, she was ready for her first break. She'd been on her feet for over twenty-six hours and she ached. As soon as she sat down and pulled out her packed dinner of two apples and a bottle of water, Bob sat down across from her and set a plate in front of her. She looked up at him.

"I can't afford this, Mr. Bob, you know that. I have my dinner."

He grinned at her. "Eat. I owe you. Saved my ass tonight, kiddo. And if you do it again next week, I'll feed you again." He laid a fifty dollar bill next to her hand. "That's for working off the clock."

"I can't take this. It was...All I did was mix some flour and milk together using your stuff. You already had the hard part finished." He pushed it back at her when she tried to give it back.

"Saved me twice that much in drinks. If they didn't have a good meal, they was gonna leave. Take it and the food with my gratitude. You deserve it."

Heather nodded and looked down at the money. She had just made Jack's field trip money.

# Chapter 4

Alex was showing the movers what to pack of his office when Brick walked in. He had a bottle of champagne and two glasses. When he popped the cork, the expensive liquid spilled more on the carpet than the glasses, but neither man seem to notice.

"So this is it." Brick toasted him with a raised glass. "I don't suppose I could change your mind and convince you to say, could I?"

Alex sat on the leather couch that was staying. "Nope. I already found me a house, my apartment is leased, and I cashed the check. You're on your own."

They had agreed to not change the name for a few months yet. At least until the last of their jobs together had been complete. All the incoming jobs and the contract with Black Security Services, the contract that had brought an end to A&B Computers, was going to be under the new name. The new name was Consolidated Hardware. Brick and his wife were sole proprietors of the new company.

"So you're really moving to Columbus," Brick said as he poured them both another glass. "Your family must be thrilled."

"They are. The house I bought is just far enough away to keep them from just dropping by, yet close enough they can drive over for a visit." Alex thought of the work he was having done on it. "Wills is overseeing most of the construction for me. Jared has agreed to do the kitchen."

Alex had just discovered he liked to cook. He had found an old cookbook at a used bookstore and had been playing with it. He still wasn't up to Jared's ability, but he was having a blast at it.

"Yeah, you said it was a big house. What the hell are you going to do with a six bedroom house?" Brick shook his head. "Lilith and I can barely fill our three-room apartment. I can't imagine one with twice that many."

He'd gotten a great deal. The housing market was great for the buyers right now. "The house needed some work. The previous owners knew they were going to lose the house to foreclosure so they trashed the place. The whole house was in bad shape, but the foundation was perfect. The bank simply wanted it off their books and I was happy to help them."

Brick snorted. "And it helps having a sister and brother-in-law that can help you with all the work too."

Alex shrugged. Yeah it did, but that wasn't all. He was actually looking forward to owning his own home. The last time he'd seen it over three weeks ago, the entire upper level, five of the bedrooms, had been gutted. There were walls in the general sense of the word, but little else. Jared had told him that it would be easier to redo than to repair.

"Wills told me last night that the carpets were being laid this week and the kitchen was being tiled today. The only rooms that are finished are the master suite and the living room."

They talked for a bit more. Alex promised that he'd keep in touch and Brick promised that as soon as he made it big, he was going to rub Alex's nose in it. He wished him all the luck in the world.

Alex was putting his bag in the car when he thought about Black Security. The hotel he'd been staying at for the past week after getting out of the apartment was being monitored by the company. The hotel's system had gone down twice since he'd been there. He hoped Brick could fix their problems, but wasn't so sure.

It wasn't that he doubted Brick's abilities to do the job; he was the best security expert he knew. It was Mikhail Black that concerned him.

There was something...shady about him, Alex decided was the best word for it. When they'd met the man and two of his guards at A&B six months ago, Alex had felt the need for a shower and a dip in some sanitizer. He'd felt dirty and somewhat contaminated after the talk. He had thought that Brick had felt the same way. But later that week, he'd changed his mind.

Mik, as he wanted everyone to call him, had said that his business was growing faster than he'd anticipated. He simply had neither the space nor the manpower to watch the extra businesses. They wanted A&B to set up the entire hardware system that would be able to record twenty-four/seven and have enough split screen monitors so they could see more at one time.

"Be the eyes we know our customers have come to expect," Mik had said. Alex thought that split screens were a waste of time and that having a busy screen meant that no one person was getting the attention they might need.

Alex had glanced at Brick when he laughed. But he covered it well when Mik had stiffened. "Isn't it better to have more people looking at four areas than sixteen as you're suggesting? I would think that having someone to keep an eye on what we treasure most would be better."

Mik disagreed. "Our men and women are trained professionals. They know what to look for and how to find even the smallest discrepancies."

Alex had seen the look that Mik had. A blast of anger burned in his eyes for a small moment, but long enough for Alex to decide he wanted nothing to do with him. Brick thought it would be the perfect way to make them a household name, and Alex wasn't so sure.

He'd done a complete background check on the man and had come up with nothing until eighteen months ago. Not even a birth certificate. When he'd tried to tell Brick, that's when they'd had their first major fight.

"You can't be serious. You think because you can't find a birth certificate that there's something wrong with the company? Hell, Alex, when I got married it took me four months to find mine. Turns out my mom hadn't filed it correctly. There can be any number of reasons why he's off the grid. I'm telling you this is the way to go."

Alex had disagreed then and still did. And when Brick had suggested that he buy him out, Alex agreed. He wanted to do things on his own for a while and this was the perfect opportunity. Besides, he wanted to part as friends, not as combatants.

As he was driving, he remembered the girl who'd hung up on him when he passed the House. He'd gone to the shop only to find Lisa there and she said that the cook, Miss Heather Laird, had already left for the day. Alex had wondered if he might have been a tad overbearing when he'd called, but he'd had a horrible headache. No excuse, but he really thought he should apologize.

Swinging into a parking space, he thought he might just pick up a few things for his family before going to his house and see if the girl was there. He was smiling when he walked inside.

~~~

Heather looked down at the paper in her hand again. She couldn't believe it. The letter had come registered mail today and she'd just now gotten the chance to open it. Looking at her grandda, she smiled again.

"Well, what are you going to do now with all your free time?" He took the letter when she handed it to him. "I knew you had it in you. Damn, girl, I've never been prouder of anything in my life. Wait until Jack sees this."

She had done so well in her classes that the online schooling she'd been taking had told her she wouldn't have to take the final. With her midterm grade and the grades of her lessons, she'd made an A in the class, giving her a 4.0 grade point average for the entire year and an overall 3.95 for her overall score. She'd done it. She was a high school graduate.

"I don't know. It seems so unreal. An A. I got an A in high school." She did a little silly dancing around the room, but couldn't seem to help it. "I couldn't have done it without you and Jack."

"'Course you couldn't." Grandda winked at her. "You did good, girl. I love you. Now put it back in the envelope so it doesn't get dirty and we'll get us a frame to put it in next payday."

She knew she shouldn't, but she really wanted to. Heather got up and decided to make something special for dinner. "Let's have pizza. I got everything we need. And Jack loves it."

The celebration lasted until she had to leave for work at the restaurant. She had let Jack stay up past his bedtime and when she left, he kissed her on the cheek when she'd gone to his room to tell him goodbye.

"I knew you could do it. I'm so proud of you, Mom. Now you have to go to college and become a great chef so you can be on that show where they kick you off if you don't make the right time." She'd smiled at him. "You'll be hosting it before the end of the first week."

"I'm sure I will." She kissed him on the forehead again. "I'm so glad you're my son. I don't know what I'd do without you."

He was yawning when he rolled over. "You'd be married to some rich guy and miserable because you'd have no one to talk to."

She was early for her shift, but it didn't matter. They were busy for a Monday night and the manager, Todd Walden, told her to clock in early. She was glad for the money and she dove right in to help out. She was waiting on a table of six customers when one of the other waitresses told her about the job as a cook.

"Seems this guy needs a housekeeper and cook to come and stay at his house. I don't know all the details, but I guess he just had this fancy house built and he don't have a wife to help keep it up." Patty, the youngest one of the group, looked excited as she gave them the news.

Bailey laughed. "Men who have fancy houses only have one thing in mind when they hire a live-in house keeper. They want themselves a live-in pussy. Mark my words, you don't want to take a job with a single man unless he getting married or he's so rich it don't matter that his dick is so tiny you don't feel a thing when he fucks you."

Heather could feel her face heat up. Bailey had been around the block a few times, she'd said. Heather had never figured out what that meant really, but she was as old as the building and had been a waitress since the first boat had come from across the Atlantic. Her words, not Heather's. There wasn't much she wouldn't discuss whether a person wanted to hear it or not.

Not that Heather was even thinking about the job. First she'd have to tell the person about Jack and she doubted very much anyone, including someone hard up, would give her a second look. She took her tray of food to the table.

Men flirted with her. Bailey had told her she was beautiful once, but Heather knew better. She was working about sixty hours a week and when she wasn't working, she was going to work or coming home. Her hair was a nondescript color of brown, her eyes a plain old blue, and her skin was so white from lack of sun she looked sort of washed out most of the time, she thought. And now, since she'd lost so much weight, she looked like a bean pole and a good stiff wind would blow her over. But the one thing she did have was boobs.

The weight loss had made them look twice as big, and no matter how much weight she did lose, her boobs remained the same. Bailey had told her once that her tits came around the corner ten minutes before Heather did. She still flushed when she thought about it.

At five-thirty, one of the day shift girls called off. As much as Heather wanted to go home and go to bed, she stayed over when Todd had asked her. She got permission to use the office phone and called Grandda.

"I have to go in too, sweetie," Grandda told her when she asked him if he could get Jack on the bus. "He'll just have to get himself going. He's a good boy, he'll do fine."

Heather almost told Todd that she couldn't do it when Jack got on the phone. "I want to do this, Mom. I'll call you when I get to the school and let you know I got there okay. I'll be very careful, okay?"

She knew he was almost ten, but she worried about him so much. After he told her another dozen times he'd be all right, she said yes.

"But you call the moment you get there. If you don't, Jack, I will come down there and yank you out of class and embarrass you. Understand?"

"Yes, ma'am. I swear." He sounded so excited she couldn't tell him no. "I have the number for the restaurant right here. I'll get there around eight. Thanks, Mom."

Three hours. She would have to wait three hours before her baby got to school and he'd call her. She didn't think she'd make it. Closing her eyes, she said a quick prayer and tried to concentrate on work.

# Chapter 5

Jack knew the rules. He'd had them drilled into his head since he could walk. The number one was not to tell anyone who he was and to scream his bloody head off if anyone tried to take him somewhere he didn't want to go. He smiled when he thought of his mother telling him that one. He'd pointed out that girls screamed and she said she didn't care what he did so long as he came home to her at the end of the day. He held his tray in his hands and looked around the bakery.

It had been three days in a row now that his mom had worked over her shift at the restaurant. She'd made so much extra money in tips that she'd told him that he could treat himself to breakfast out. His grandpa Tom was getting more hours, too, at his job. They assured him that it wasn't going to be much longer and the money would be good. And he called her every morning when he got to school just like he'd promised.

The second morning had been a little tense. He had tried dialing her four times before he finally got her. She told him that her boss was on the phone trying to replace the girl who had quit. Jack had been just about ready to walk to the restaurant to tell her he'd made it when she came to the phone.

"I'm so sorry. Are you going to be late to class now?"

He looked up at the big clock in the hall when she'd asked. "No, ma'am. I have about five minutes. I was scared you were gonna be mad at me if I didn't call."

"I know."

She sounded close to tears and he didn't want her to cry anymore. So he put as much humor in his voice as he could. "I was going to catch myself a taxi and go down there and yank you bald. You'd look pretty silly waiting tables with no hair." He grinned when she laughed a little. "Of course then maybe that Todd guy would leave you alone."

She laughed again, then sighed. "Thanks, buddy. I needed that. I'll see you tonight. Be careful and have fun today."

"Mom, I'm at school. Nobody has fun at school."

After that, he wasn't required to call her unless something happened. Which it hadn't, not really he supposed. It was just the normal stuff, kids giving him a hard time because of his clothes or because of his grades, which were always the best in the class. It bothered him more about the grades than his clothes, but then he wasn't trying to make the cover of any girly magazine.

He knew his mom worked here as the cook. He also knew that she had been the one to make the blueberry muffin on his plate. What he didn't know was where he was supposed to sit to eat it. Every table in the place was filled. He saw the man sitting with the laptop on his table and walked toward him, keeping an eye on the other people in the dining area as well.

"Excuse me, mister, can I sit down, please?" Nothing. Whatever was on the computer had the guy's full attention. He tried again. "Mister. Do you think it would be okay if I eat my breakfast here?" The guy didn't move except for his fingers over the keyboard.

Jack looked around the room again and decided when the man by the door winked at him, Jack was going to sit with this guy and nobody else. Maybe the guy was too busy to notice one kid anyway. He put his tray down as quietly as he could and sat across from him. He was pulling off the paper from the muffin when the guy's phone went off.

~~~

Alex looked at the kid across from him. He didn't say anything, but watched him finish unwrapping his muffin and then fold the wrapper into a neat square before he picked up his knife. Alex watched as he cut the thing into four pieces before he spoke.

"Usually people wait to be invited before they sit down. Of course, I could be wrong about the way things are done in this part of Ohio, but I don't think so."

"I tried, but you didn't hear me. I asked you twice. I have to catch the bus in a bit and you can hog the table back up if you want."

Alex raised a brow. The kid had a smart mouth on him, that was for sure. Now he was taking the knife and cutting the muffin's four pieces into four more, all in precise sizes. When he was finished, he laid the knife across his plate and put his paper napkin on his lap.

"I could have sat with the lady with the eight hundred kids, I guess. But I was afraid she'd gather me up with the rest of her brood and I'd be gone for a month before she noticed me."

Alex looked over at the woman with the four children. They were very rowdy and loud and Alex thought the kid was right in thinking she'd never notice him. One of her children was on the floor asleep and the woman just kept talking on her cell phone.

"And you picked me because I have no kids? For all you know, I could be waiting on someone." He didn't know why he didn't just tell the kid to get lost, but he was enjoying himself too much.

"You were too absorbed in whatever you're doing on your computer to notice a kid. I doubt very much you were waiting on anyone. Even if you were, how do you know they didn't already come and leave because you didn't notice them?"

Alex had to bite the inside of his mouth to keep from laughing at his answer. "That still doesn't mean...what about that guy by the door? Why not go pick on him?" Alex didn't like the way the guy was looking at them, but decided he wasn't going to say anything.

"You mean the guy who looks like a pedophile? I think I saw him on the news last week." The kid turned and looked at the guy in question. "Yeah, I think he'd murdered like seventeen people before he disappeared off the face of the earth. No, you were my safest bet."

Alex threw back his head and laughed. "You're all right, kid. My name is Alexander. And you would be?"

"Not telling you who I am." The kid picked up his tray as he stood. "Thanks for the use of your table, Mr. Alexander. You can go back to your work."

"Wait. You can't go." The kid quirked a brow back at him. "What I mean is the guy, the pedophile, he might follow you. Let me at least walk you to the bus stop. If you don't trust me, you can…you can ask the owner of this shop about me. She'll vouch for me."

The kid looked at the man by the door that had stood when he did. Alex wasn't sure how he was going to do it, but he wasn't going to let the kid walk out of here alone. He'd like to find the boy's parents and tell them what could happen to a kid on the streets alone now days.

"I swear to you I'm not going to touch you or do anything to you. I just want to make sure you get on the bus all right." Caroline came out into the dining area just then and Alex waved her over. "This is my friend Caroline. She owns this establishment. I don't want this young man to leave here alone to catch the bus. Would you tell him I'm harmless? Please?"

He wasn't sure she thought he was serious until she looked at the kid. "You couldn't ask for a better guy in your corner. Saved my butt the other day." Caroline ruffled the kid's head as she went by him.

The kid looked torn. He kept looking at the man who had just walked out the door and back at Alex. He knew the moment the kid decided to let him come with him. But it was still undecided if he trusted him or not.

"I have to catch the bus on the corner. If I'm not there, the bus will know to call my mom." Alex nodded, knowing the kid was lying to him, but thought it was very smart of him too. "Okay, but you do one thing that makes me think you're as bad as the guy on the corner and I'll…I'll scream bloody murder."

Alex nodded again and stood. He'd remained seated until then because he was sure his size would have terrified the already scared kid. He left his computer on the table and moved to the other side. Caroline said she'd keep an eye on it for him.

"Geez, mister, you're huge." The kid backed up three steps and Alex was sure he was going to bolt. "I guess I should have looked harder before I sat down."

"Maybe my size will keep the guy outside from bothering you if he thinks we're together." Alex grabbed his coat and looked out the door to see the guy on the other side of the street.

"I'm not dating you, you're walking me to the bus stop. Let's not get ahead of ourselves here." The kid took a napkin off the holder on the table and wiped his area down, then he took the tray to the trash can and put his trash in, what little bit there was. He handed Lisa the tray with a smile. "That was very delicious. Thank you very much." Lisa looked up at Alex with a stunned look on her face.

Most of the kids they got in here were rude and obnoxious. The other day there had been a food fight and he had helped Caroline toss them out. One of the kids, some rich punk, told Alex that he'd be back with his lawyer. Alex took out his business card and told the kid to have him call him instead. He hadn't been called nor had anyone showed up.

The kid in front of him was a handsome boy. He was tall, but since Alex didn't have a clue how old he was, he couldn't say if he was tall for his age. His clothes were clean if not a bit worn. His coat was a little tight on him and Alex knew he'd be out of it before real winter hit. He had on gloves and a skull cap and both those looked a little big, but otherwise he was covered.

His eyes were a startling shade of gray. Not really gray, Alex thought, but a slate color. His blond hair was long, just over his collar, and it curled slightly. His nose was a classic one, and the high cheekbones told of good breeding. Alex grinned when he thought of what the kid would say to that. He was sure it would be a lot.

"So," Alex started when they were about halfway down the block, "you going to tell me your name? I told you mine."

"No, sir. That could be your alias and you could be Attila the Hun for all I know, or at least related to him." They were at the crosswalk when the kid looked up at him. "No offense, but my mom would flay my skin off me if she knew I was doing this. If I told you my name, I might as well just walk in front of the next car. It might be quicker."

Alex laughed. He liked this kid and wondered about his mother. She must be a hell of a woman to raise a smart-mouthed kid like him and still have a sense of humor too. He was crossing the street when he noticed the man again. He walked up beside the kid to shield him from the stranger.

"Kid, your mom is a walk in the park compared to mine. She once hosed me and my sister down in the kitchen because we were fighting. She has a wicked way of making you toe the line without raising her voice."

"My mom told the electric guy the other day that she'd sooner eat a skunk raw than to go out with him. I believed her. The guy...I think he thinks she's nuts." Alex was amused to think of this spunky kid being afraid of his mom. "This is my stop. Thank you, mister."

"I'll wait until the bus comes." Alex saw the kid glance back to the stranger. He was pleased to see the kid was aware too. "I won't leave you."

"He followed me here. And he's taking pictures. Do you suppose he uses them for sex?" The kid looked back at the stranger on the corner again. "I don't know him. And I don't want to either."

"He won't come near you. When you get off the bus at school, are there other people around? Adults?" Alex stared at the man, trying to get as much detail as he could. Suddenly, the stranger put his cell phone away and moved down the street.

"Yes, sir. Teachers." He heard the kid sigh. "He's gone now. Thanks for walking me here."

"No problem. But I'll stay until the bus comes." There were enough people milling around that Alex stepped closer to the kid. He didn't know why he was getting involved and was a little surprised at it. He'd been doing that a lot lately and was starting to think he should have found something better to do with his time.

"This is my bus," the kid said as he pulled out a card. "Thanks again, sir. I really appreciate you letting me sit at your table and then this. It was very kind of you."

Alex stuck out his hand and was happy when the kid took it. When he turned away then turned back, Alex could see the kid was struggling with something.

"It was my pleasure, really. I needed the exercise and it's not too cold out yet for me to get a cold. You have a great day at school, kid."

"My name is Jack," he said as he walked up the steps and onto the bus. The door was closed before he could say anything back.

# Chapter 6

Heather was exhausted. It had been five days now since she'd been working the extra half shift in the morning and wasn't sure she could do it much more. The tips were great and so long as she was there, she wasn't as tired because they were so busy. But now, standing with her hands in bread dough, she wasn't so sure. When the timer went off, she went to the oven, pulled out a pan of cookies, and put them on the cooling rack. While she was standing there, Lisa came back to get some supplies.

"Out of sugar cookies again. And a customer wants to know if you'll be making some Christmas ones soon. I tried to tell him it was only November, but he just smiled at me. Moron." Lisa started putting the sugar dusted cookies she needed on a tray as she continued. "Also, Mom wants to talk to you later if you have time. She's got some great news."

Heather nodded. She hoped that she was hiring another cook, but quickly changed her mind. The extra money she was making wouldn't be extra if she lost her job. When Lisa was gone, she moved to the bread again.

She couldn't remember when she'd had her last good night's sleep. Probably since before Jack was born. She grinned when she thought of him this morning telling her he was going to be in the Christmas pageant at school. She closed her eyes for a second and drifted off. When the alarm went off again, she nearly screamed. She had actually fallen asleep standing up. When she pulled the first batch of cakes out of the oven, she grabbed her bottle of water and stepped outside.

It was mid-November now and it was feeling it. She knew she had to get to the store and get Jack a coat before much longer. He was growing so much. Then there were the presents she wanted to get him for Christmas.

Last year had been rough on them. Grandda had had a very bad cold and all their extra money had gone to medicine for him. She'd had to work some parties that she didn't care for just to make the rent. Nothing bad in the parties; she just hated drunks. Laughing, she thought about her Friday night job and went back in. The frigid air had made her feel more awake. She was taking out the next batch of cookies when a man walked in the kitchen.

"You're not allowed back here. This is the kitchen and the pastries and stuff are out there." She pointed to the door he'd walked through. "I'm sure whatever you looking for is out there."

He grinned and Heather felt her belly clench up. *Man, to have a man smile at you like that could hurt a girl*, she thought. He was gorgeous and sexy-looking standing there leaning against the doorway. She felt herself flush when she thought of sex. It had been years...She closed that thought off immediately.

The man was tall, really tall, and he looked like he could keep a girl happy all night. She flushed again when that thought popped in her head. She turned around to her dough. *Christ, love a duck.* She must be more tired than she thought. His laughter made her think he knew just what she'd been thinking. And for whatever reason, that pissed her off. "You need to go away. There's no reason for you to be back here." The timer went off again. "I'll have to ask you to leave."

"Smells good back here. You must be the baker. I'm Alex." She could hear him move, but ignored him. "Can I help you with that?"

When he started for her, she moved and the bread shifted on the pan. When it did, she had to shift it to keep the bread from falling to the floor. In doing so, she felt the hot edge of it touch her forearm. She couldn't help the cry of pain, but she didn't drop the pan.

When she got it on the rack, she rushed to the sink to run cold water over it. She could feel the tears spilling down and she had to bite her lip to keep from screaming at the man.

"I need you to go to the front," she stated calmly when she was jerked around. "Hey, what do you think you're doing? Let me go."

He growled at her to hush and pulled her injured arm to him. She could smell him now, expensive. He had on something that probably cost more than she made in a week. And that made her mad.

"Let me go you baboon. I want to put water on it. If you'd just gone to the front like I told you I wouldn't have gotten burned. Now let me go."

"If you want to blame me then go right ahead, but you should have let me help you. I was trying to be a gentleman." He was patting a towel over the burn when she looked down.

"Oh shit. I'm going to be sick." She jerked from him and rushed to the bathroom. She had just locked the door and was leaning over the toilet when she threw up.

Hard heaves came up from her belly and burned her throat. It was always like this when she was hurt, worse when Jack or Grandda was hurt. She just couldn't stand seeing open wounds. When she thought she was finished, she stood up and looked in the mirror, careful not to look at her arm. Turning on the cold water, she stared at the woman looking back at her.

Who was she? Heather had been working so hard for so long, she didn't know her any more. She looked like one of those women she saw in Wal-Mart at two in the morning. Too tired to wear makeup and wearing jammies. Heather didn't own any makeup, but she refused wear jammies in public. With a splash of cold water to refresh her, she stepped out of the bathroom. It was too much to hope Mr. Expensive would be gone.

~~~

Alex had called Lisa back to tell her what had happened to the girl. She said her name was Heather. Lisa said she'd call her mom and have her come in. He'd found her coat near the door and was holding it when Heather looked at him.

"Come on, I'll take you to the hospital. Lisa is calling her mom to have her come and finish what you have going." He held out her coat for her to slip on. "Come on, miss, that needs to be looked at."

"I'm not going anywhere with you. And I'm certainly not going to the hospital. You need to go back up front and leave me to my job." She walked past him to the paper towel rack and pulled off several sheets. "It's just a burn. It's part and parcel of the job. Now if you'll excuse me."

He watched her wrap the sheets gently around her arm, not looking at the area until she had it covered. He still held her coat as he walked toward her.

"Maybe you didn't hear me say we were going. I didn't ask. Put on your coat and let's go. I have things I have to do today and they don't—"

"Then go do them. I'm not stopping you. In case you hadn't noticed, I'm a big girl and can take care of myself. Been doing it awhile now."

He'd noticed she was a big girl. It would be hard not to. And a beautiful one at that. He couldn't decide if it was the blue eyes or the sadness in them that had him wanting to pull her into his arms. And he wasn't even sure he'd live to talk about it if he tried. She was a prickly thing.

"I want you to put this damn coat on and let me take you to get that wound looked at. I'm not kidding, Heather. Either we do this easy or we do this hard. Understand me?"

She looked at him for several seconds, studying him, he supposed, when she threw back her head and laughed. She walked to the oven when the timer went off and opened it. Testing whatever was in there, she closed it up and put another five minutes on the timer.

"I spoke to you on the phone once. About a month ago. You were demanding then too. Called me a liar. Twice. I didn't like you then and I don't like you any better now that we meet face to face."

The girl on the phone. The one he'd come by to apologize to. He'd never seen her before today, but he'd heard a great deal about her. He walked to her, holding out her coat again. "Well, you're really going to hate me now. As of yesterday, I'm part owner of this place and as such, I'm taking you to the hospital. Now put the fucking coat on or so help me I will bend you over my knee, blister your ass good, and take you anyway."

He watched with fascination as her face went from happy that she'd remembered him to violent in a heartbeat or two. He had never seen anything so beautiful and sexy in his life and wondered fleetingly if she put that much passion in making love. He felt his cock twitch thinking about it. But when she stepped toward him with a look in her eye that he'd seen his sister have, he backed up.

"Why you overbearing, pigheaded swine. You think you can just waltz your ass back here and order me around like I'm...like I'm a child? Well I'm not going anywhere with you. I quit." She tore off her apron and threw it at him. "You can take this job and shove it up your bottom. I won't work for you."

She was nearly to the door when he grabbed for her. He didn't mean to grab her arm, but when she snatched the coat out of his hand and moved, he saw red. When she screamed, he let her go immediately. She crumpled to the floor and would have hit her head on the sink, but he caught her before she did. Caroline came in just as he was lifting her up.

It took him five minutes to explain what had happened. He felt like shit and hated himself more in that moment than he'd ever had in his life. He was putting her in the back of his car, talking to Caroline as he strapped her in.

"I'm so sorry. I hurt her arm and when she started to leave...she quit. I'll take care of that. I'll give her a raise or whatever. I'm so sorry, Caroline."

"Just call me when you get her there. And Alex, you'd better make her stay or our deal is off. I love this girl and I don't think she has a pot to piss in and she can't lose this job. I know…well, we'll talk about her when you get her back."

Heather came around as he was putting her on the gurney at the hospital. She was sobbing now and he wanted to comfort her. But the emergency team that came to get her from him wouldn't let him near her. The receptionist stopped him before he sat down.

"You'll need to fill out the paper work for you wife, sir. Then I'll take you back to her. Poor thing. She'll be all right."

Alex started to tell her that she wasn't his wife, but knew that if he did, he'd never get to go back. And he needed to see her again. Taking the clipboard that she handed him, he went to find a seat. The place was nearly empty so he took the one furthest from the desk.

Name. He had no idea other than Heather. He wrote that down and skipped to the next question while he pulled out his cell to call and ask Caroline. He was at the part where her address needed to go when he realized he had no service. Taking a deep breath, he started filling it out with a mixture of her name and his information. He was quite satisfied when he handed it back to the woman at the desk.

"Okay Mr. James, let me take you back to see your wife now. If they have any questions, I'm sure they'll know where to find you." He looked down at the name he'd put on the paper when she did. "Heather James, what a lovely name."

When he was shown her room, he hesitated. She was going to be more pissed than she had been at the bakery.

He took a deep breath and walked around the curtain. What he saw when he did made him whimper a little. Christ, she was lovely.

Her back was to him and naked. She had taken off her shirt and her bra was unhooked. Her jeans were still on, but they were low-riders and he could see the colorful tattoo she had at the base of her spine. It was a rose in the middle with swirls on either side of it. It was about three inches high and about five inches wide. He found himself wondering just how far those blue and green lines went down and wanted to taste his way there. When she turned toward him, he found both his mouth dry as a bone and his heart pounding in his chest. He was a dead man.

"They told me I could come back to be with you." He walked to her slowly. "The nurse at the desk said the doctor would be in soon." He was babbling. He watched her carefully for any signs of murder or weapons. When she started to slip her shirt back over her head, he took it from her and tossed it on the chair.

"I'm going home. I can't afford to be here. And I certainly don't want you here." She'd been crying and he felt bad. "Don't you ever listen?"

"Not really. Has anyone looked at your arm yet?" She was still holding the gown in front of her. "I think you're supposed to put that on, not hold it like that."

"I would, but there's a strange man in my room. I want you to give me back my shirt and go away. I'm having a really sh...crappy day and I just want to finish it."

"No." He grinned at her. "It's been shitty. You can say it. Let me help you put this on properly."

She smacked his hands away from her. He wasn't deterred by either the glare or the slaps.

"I bet your wife wants to murder you on a daily basis. I know I would." She stilled when he lifted her chin up and looked her in the face. "What?"

"You should know something." He looked at her lips when her tongue darted out and moistened them. His train of thought completely vanished. He looked up into her eyes.

"Know what?" Her voice had gone husky and low. When her tongue came out again, he lowered his head to hers. He found that he wanted to kiss her, taste her in the worst way.

He brushed his mouth over hers softly. He already knew she was going to taste as good as she looked. When he went back again a little firmer, she signed. Since he didn't feel anything sharp poking him, Alex gave in and kissed her.

He was drowning in her. She tasted like hot sex and honey. When her mouth opened under his, he pulled her closer, careful of her arm. His hand met warm flesh and he groaned. Moving his hand up her ribs, he felt the heavy weight of her breast just beneath his thumb and rubbed it along the underside. Her groan had him cupping her breast in his hand and lifting it up. His cock leapt to attention at the hard peak that he encountered.

"Heather James? Excuse me, are you Heather James?" He lifted his head at the question and nearly dipped his head back for more.

Her eyes were closed and her lips were swollen from his kiss. Her breast still filled his hand and he wanted to taste it, but the voice on the other side of the curtain spoke again.

"I'm Doctor Phillips. I've come to have a look at your burn, Mrs. James. Are you dressed yet?"

Alex watched her become aware by degrees. Her eyes opened slowly and her tongue came out and licked along her lips as if to savor his taste. He groaned when she smiled.

"If you do that again, I'm going to be laying us both back on this bed and damn the doctor." Her eyes popped open. "Christ, I want you."

"What do you think you're...back up. What, doctor?" she snapped at him as she shoved him away.

"Me, Mrs. James. I'm Doctor Phillips. Let's have a look at that arm shall we?"

# Chapter 7

Heather listened to the doctor with half an ear. The man behind her had her full attention and she didn't like it one bit. The nerve of the man to kiss her like she was...like she was someone who wanted to be kissed. And she didn't, not really. She didn't think. Nor did she want to think about her name linked to his.

But the kiss was amazing. Every time she thought of his mouth over hers she tingled everywhere. She tried to clamp down on that thought. And when he'd touched her nipple...she flushed again just thinking about it. Well, she thought, he'd better back off now. She wasn't in as much pain thanks to the pain pill they'd given her.

"You should make an appointment to see your family doctor as soon as possible. If you'd like, we can make the appointment for you from here. Doctors always have room when we call them," Doctor Phillips said to her with a smile.

"I can do it. I have to...I need to find his number." *And find a doctor too,* she thought. "I'll call him as soon as I get back to work."

"Oh no, Mrs. James. You shouldn't go back to work. With the medication we've given you, you might want to go home and rest for a few days. I'm sure your husband can take care of your boss for you." She turned to glare at her "husband" when he laughed. "He can make him understand that you need your rest. And I'd like to see you put on a few more pounds as well. You seem to be very underweight and that can contribute to you being able to fight any infection you might get. Burns can be very serious."

"I assure you, doctor, I'm going to handle my boss. Thank you for your time." She pulled the gown out in the front and hoped no one noticed her nipples were poking through the thin material. "I'll just get dressed now."

There was tug of war between her and Mr. James, but in the end, he gave her the bag with her clothes in it. She'd been taken down to x-ray for whatever reason and when she'd returned, all of her things were in a white plastic bag instead of on the bed where she'd left them. When she came out the bathroom, a nurse was there with her paperwork and Mr. James. She ignored him.

She was just signing off that she understood what she needed to do in case of infection when she asked where the billing office was.

"It's on the second floor. But your insurance should cover this, Mrs. James. And we have your address to send anything that it doesn't."

"But I don't have any ins—"

"Come on, honey. If you're all signed out, let me take you home and get you to bed." She shivered when she thought of getting into bed with this man. "And if you're really good, I'll let you be on top," he whispered to her as he put his arm around her.

Her entire body responded. She wanted to bash him in the head with the nearest object and snuggle under the protective feelings of his arm around her. She stopped dead in her tracks when she realized that.

"You need to step back from me or so help me they will be putting you in a body bag before I get to the door." He did take a step back, but not far enough for her comfort. "I don't have any insurance. What did you tell her to make her think...you put me on yours."

"Yes. And before you get your panties in a twist about it, I've already made arrangements with my insurance company. They know that I'm good for it so when the bills come to them, I will simply pay them. End of story."

"I want you to give them to me. They're my bills and I'll pay them." She didn't know how she was going to manage that, but she would if she had to take another five jobs to do it. "I don't know why you'd do something so stupid, but it was not necessary."

They were outside now and the wind was biting through her coat. She hadn't been able to put her arm in the sleeve, but she did manage to get it wrapped around her. When he tried tugging her along, she stopped.

"My car is over here. And I warmed it up. The sooner I get you out of the cold, the sooner you can stop shivering." He pulled again, but she didn't budge...not too much anyway.

"I'm not going with you. I have to get home. And I have to get back to work." She thought of Jack and wondered what time it was. "If you'll just make sure you give the bills to Miss Caroline, I'll take care of them."

"Why are you so damned stubborn? Never mind, I don't care. Get in the car, Heather, and I'll take you home. It's the least I can do since I'm the one who caused you to get hurt in the first place." He stood in front of her like a wall. "Am I going to have to carry you again?"

"You most certainly will not." When she turned to go to the street to see if she could catch a bus, he moved in front of her. "Do you mind? I've already told you I'm not—"

The rest of what she was going to say came out as a squeal. He picked her up in his arms as if she weighed nothing. When he gave her a little toss, she wrapped her arm around his shoulder and hung on. When he put her down, she was going to kick him in the balls.

"I can feel you thinking of all sorts of things you're going to do to me and none of them are as pleasurable as the kiss we shared in the hospital. If I were you, I'd keep my feet and hands to myself until we can get to somewhere more private. I'm thinking your bed or mine."

Suddenly, she was dizzy. Not just dizzy, but going to throw up dizzy. The doctor had mentioned that she'd feel the effects of the medicine they'd given her in about half an hour, but she was sure it didn't wait. When her head rolled back on her shoulders, she heard someone shout her name then nothing.

~~~

Terrified out of his mind, Alex sat her on the seat of his car and reached for her pulse. He'd never seen anyone go out like that. She had been spitting mad one second and out cold the next. When he found her pulse beating steadily, he leaned his head on her shoulder. Then he looked up at her.

Christ, she was beautiful. He knew the doctor was right in saying she was underweight but it didn't take from her. The blue of her eyes had him breathless and when she was mad like she'd been since he first laid eyes on her, they were dark, like they'd been when she looked up at him from their kiss. Her skin was so fair he wondered if she would ever be able to walk in the bright sun without burning, and the dozen or so freckles across her nose made his mouth water.

"Christ, you have me wanting you because of a few freckles across your nose." He pulled the seat belt across her and couldn't help but cup her breast again.

They were large and full, firm and soft. He wanted to pull up her blouse and suckle at the hard nipple he could see even through her bra. Shutting her door before he did something stupid…or stupider, he adjusted his cock again for the eightieth time since he'd kissed her and got into his car.

Now what? He supposed he could take her to his house, but was reasonably sure she really would hurt him. He hadn't picked up her purse so he didn't have a clue where she lived. He thought about calling Caroline and asking where she lived, but he wasn't sure he wanted Heather on her own turf yet. He thought about his sister, but knew she was at a job site and then thought of the one person he knew would understand. Putting the car into gear, he pulled out his cell phone and called his mom.

"Hello, dear. I was just thinking about you. There is the loveliest girl that lives next door to us. You really should meet her."

He glanced over at the woman next to him. "No thanks. Mom, I have this problem…well, she's not a problem." He glanced over at her again. "Not yet at least. She's going to be really mad when she wakes up, but that could be at least another hour yet. I hope."

"Alexander, what are you talking about? You have a woman you've rendered unconscious. I do believe there are laws forbidding that sort of treatment." He could hear her laughter and smiled. "Please tell me you aren't so desperate for a date you've taken to drugging women."

"No. Well, not really. The doctor is the one who...Mom, do you think I can bring her to your house? I'm pretty sure she won't kill me with you there and I'll explain when I get there." He hoped so anyway.

"Of course. But I do expect a full explanation when you arrive. Shall I call someone for her? Or for you?"

"No, ma'am. Not yet at any rate. I'll be there in ten minutes."

Alex had plenty of time to think while he drove. This was so out of the ordinary for him that he really couldn't blame his mother for being suspicious. He'd never had to beg a woman for kisses. Hell, he'd never had to even ask. Women just found him to be irresistible. Until this one. She hated him on the spot. Of course he'd done nothing to make her like him. He'd called her a liar and he'd made her burn her arm. Then on top of that, he'd ripped open the burn bad enough to make her have to seek medical treatment. By the time he pulled up in the front gate at his parents' house, he was no closer to figuring out what made this girl so different and so hard to not want than he'd been when he'd picked her up at the bakery.

He picked her up out of the car and carried her into the house. His mom was there waiting as was his dad. His dad was laughing and his mom was scowling at him.

"For heaven's sake, Alexander, what have you done? I thought you were kidding when you said you were bringing a woman...oh the poor dear. Take her up to the guest room and I'll come with you."

Heather started to come around about halfway up the stairs. She stretched in his arms and smiled up at him. His heart took a serious skip and he had to stop moving or fall. She wrapped her arm around him again and snuggled deep into his neck before he could catch his breath. Then breathing became impossible. When she pressed her mouth to his, Alex was lost.

He knew she was dreaming. There was no way she'd come this willingly into his arms without the drugs. But damn, it felt good to have her there. When she moaned against his mouth, Alex let her legs fall as she adjusted herself around him. Everything around them faded away as she slid her tongue along his and wrapped her fingers in his hair. His mom's "oh my" had him wishing he'd taken Heather to his house. She stiffened in his arms and nearly launched herself away from him.

"What do you think you're doing? You can't...where am I?"

"My parents' house. And you kissed me first so don't go blaming me for that." She looked ready to explode and he wanted to pull her to him and start again. "You were asleep and I didn't know where you lived."

"So you brought me here? And kissed me? Are you...I need to go." She made to move away from him and he stopped her. Without waiting for her approval, which he was sure she wouldn't give, he scooped her up in his arms. "Put me down. I don't feel so well."

He carried her up to the bedroom and laid her down. When she didn't protest, he knew she was sick. Going to the bathroom, he wet one of the hand towels there, took it to her, and put it gently on her eyes.

"Alexander?"

He looked over at his parents. "She got burned at work this morning and then we had a...thing and I tore open the blisters. The ER doctor gave her something for pain and it hit her when we were getting in the car."

His mom stood there and looked at him. He couldn't even begin to wonder what was going through her mind. She finally reached out and brought the door nearly closed before she spoke. "Call us if you need us." Then the door closed.

Alex looked down at Heather then sat on the bed beside her. She started to sit up, but he simply pushed her back. When she tried it again, he rolled over her and covered her with his body. "This is nice." It was too. Her body fit beneath his as though she'd been made to be there.

"Let me up right now." She pushed against his shoulders. "I mean it, Mr. James. This is no longer funny."

He took both her hands in his and pulled them up to the head board. "First of all, my name is Alexander or Alex, whichever you prefer. Secondly…" He leaned down and nipped at her neck where the shoulder met. "You calling me Mr. James when I bury myself deep inside of you could be scary."

He rocked into her. He tried to be gentle, to be slow, but she tasted so good, felt so good, that he found he wanted…no, he needed more. He took her mouth and devoured her.

Running his hand up her waist, he grasped the hem of her shirt in his fingers and worked them beneath the thin cotton. Moving his hand up, he skimmed hot skin, felt her muscles ripple beneath his touch. When he encountered her bra, he slid his fingers under it and filled his hand once again with her. She arched into him then ripped her mouth from his as she threw back her head and moaned deep, dark, and primal.

Moving his head down to her ribs, Alex bit then laved the tiny wound with his tongue while he moved the lace from what he wanted. Her. Her and her hard nipple. When she was free, Alex took the hardened peak into his mouth and suckled.

"Please," she moaned as her fingers wrapped into his hair and her legs wrapped around his hips. She rode him, rode him as hard as he did her. He wanted her now, wanted her forever.

He froze. Forever?

Alex rolled to his back and away from her to the other side of the bed. He'd only just met her today. This couldn't be happening. Throwing his arm over his eyes, he tried to get a grip.

What the hell had he been doing? What had they nearly done? He looked over at her when he felt the bed shift to see her getting up and moving to the door. She was adjusting her clothes. It took her slamming out the door when she left the room before he realized she was leaving.

Alex leapt from the bed to catch her. She was about halfway down the stairs when he caught up with her and when he did, he quickly took two steps back when she turned.

"Leave me alone, damn it. Being with you is like being a yo-yo on a string." She sat on the stairs. "You have me so churned up inside I'm not sure if I want to beat you senseless or strip you naked and have you."

Alex flushed. He knew just how she felt. When his father chuckled coming up the stairs, he knew they'd heard her.

"I'd like to go back to the bakery, please. If someone could please take me, I'd very much appreciate it." When he stepped forward, she practically snarled at him. "Don't you dare. I swear to you if you kiss me again, I'm going to hit you over the head with something."

His dad burst out laughing and his mother was trying her best not to join him. Alex didn't see anything the least bit funny about any of this and couldn't understand what the hell they were laughing about.

"You are suppose to be going—" She lifted her hand and he shut up.

"Could someone please take me back to the bakery? I have a job there that needs finishing." She smiled at his dad and he nodded.

"I'll take you, dear. Let me get my coat. Alex, why don't you stay here and keep your mother company?" Alex thought he heard his dad mumble, "it might be safer for you," but wasn't sure. They were out the door before he could get a word out.

He looked over at his mom who was smiling at him. He didn't care for that smile and wished like hell he'd taken Heather to his house. This one had lunatics in it.

"So, you've been kissing her, have you? She seems like a girl who...well, knows her own mind." Alex wanted to glare at her, but couldn't take another woman threatening him again today. "Who is she?"

"My wife."

# Chapter 8

Jack looked at his mom again. She was acting strange. He'd never seen her hurt before for one thing, and she was madder than a hornet too. Jack had never actually seen a hornet before, but he'd heard his grandpa Tom say that before about somebody he worked with and decided if they looked like this then he wanted nothing to do with them. She started pacing again when he saw the tears.

"Mom, why don't you sit down? You look like you could use a rest." She actually looked like she could use a good long nap, but he wisely kept that to himself. "I'll get you a cup of tea."

While he busied himself with the kettle, he kept hoping Grandpa Tom would come home. He'd know what to do. When she blew her nose again, Jack went over and hugged her. She hugged him back.

"Oh Jack, what have I done?" He didn't know what she meant, but patted her on the shoulder as she continued. "That man is going to drive me insane. And if he thinks he can kiss me whenever he wants just because he—"

"Some man kissed you?" he shouted. "That's just nasty. Gross, Mom, no wonder you're all mad and stuff. Did he use his tongue and everything?"

He knew he'd gone just a bit too far when she raised both her brows at him. He wondered if she thought he didn't know about sex and then decided maybe he'd better not ask. She seemed sort of…unhinged today.

"He most certainly did not." Then she frowned. "Not really. He…he did, but I didn't like it. Not really."

"You said that twice. Who kissed you and why?" He didn't want to think about his mom having anyone kiss her but him. "Is he the one that hurt you?"

"No, he didn't hurt me. It was an accident. Why did he kiss me?" She got up and started pacing the tiny kitchen. When the kettle started screaming that it was done, she made them both a cup of hot water. He hated hot tea and he was sure she knew it, but he thought if he got answers, he'd drink both their cups.

"I don't have any idea why he kissed me. Maybe he's deranged or something." Jack liked the sound of that. "He said he wanted to kiss me again." He didn't care so much for that.

"Why? I mean, I guess it's okay if you're married or something when you have to kiss a girl, but gross, why would you do it on purpose? And want to do it again?" He picked up his cup and blew on it, stalling. "I seen people do it in movies, but I don't see the big deal."

"I suppose you'll change your mind when you get older," she told him as she sat down with her cup.

He highly doubted that. Girls were okay and he liked kissing his mom, but girls? "I guess kissing a guy is different than when you kiss me, huh?"

"Very. Men and women don't always kiss because they're married either. Though I haven't been on a date in a long time, I guess they still do that." She got up and pulled down the cookie tin. "But I would guess your grandpa Tom knows more about that than either of us."

Jack thought his grandpa Tom knew everything. He was sometimes fuzzy on the details, but he knew a lot. He decided to ask him about kissing when he got the chance. He didn't think he'd get the same answers he got from his mom, but he'd bet they'd be more colorful. Jack thought he'd ask his new friend Mr. Alex when he saw him again. If he saw him again.

Jack hadn't told him mom about the stranger or his grandpa Tom. He did tell him about Mr. Alex. He'd told him how he'd shared a table with him and they'd had a good time. He didn't want to tell him that Mr. Alex had walked him to the bus stop, afraid that his grandpa Tom would think he was a baby, but he hadn't said that at all.

"Good for you. It's always nicer to take a stroll when you have a buddy with you. You can watch each other's backs while you do it. You say he's a friend of Miss Caroline? Well, probably knows about your mom then." Grandpa Tom was quiet for a minute. "Don't think I'd mention him to your mom. She's a mite protective of you and would probably make you stay away from him. But listen, boy, he touches you or does anything that has you uncomfortable, you tell Miss Caroline and beat your ass home, hear?"

"Yes, sir. I will."

Jack looked over at the paper on the fridge with everyone's schedule on it. He was thrilled to see his grandpa Tom had to work again in the morning and wondered if his mom would work over too. He was torn about that. He wanted her home to rest, but he wouldn't mind spending some time with Mr. Alex too.

She got up from the table and started making dinner. He had to get his homework done before he'd be allowed to watch television so he pulled his book bag up on the table. He was just starting on his math when he heard his grandpa Tom's keys in the door.

After dinner was cleaned up, he and his grandpa Tom sat down to watch some TV. His mom had gone to take her nap and he looked over at the older man when a commercial came on.

"Grandpa Tom, I have something to tell you. Please don't tell Mom." He had to confess. It was weighing heavily on his mind.

"Can't make a call on that until you tell me what it is that's eating you up. If it's about your momma's burn then you can rest assured I'll make sure she keeps it clean and dry."

Jack knew he would, and so would he. "No, sir. It's about the man, Mr. Alex, and the real reason he walked me to the bus this morning."

Grandpa Tom turned off the TV and looked at him. He didn't say anything, but Jack knew that he'd have plenty to say once he heard. So he told him everything including the man taking pictures.

"He was across the street when the bus came up. Mr. Alex, he walked in front of me the whole time like he didn't want him to see me. I wasn't scared when I was with him, but...well, I was about the man. It was like one of those movies where the kid is watched to see if he has a pattern then he gets snatched."

"You say this man, Mr. Alex, he saw him too?" Jack nodded. "You didn't approach the man, did you? Say anything to him?" Jack shook his head. "You don't either."

Grandpa Tom sat back on the couch and closed his eyes. The room was dark, but Jack could see well enough to see that he wasn't asleep. When he turned to Jack, he knew it was going to be something he didn't like.

"I'm going to meet you down there tomorrow and have a talk with this man." Jack started to protest; he didn't want his grandpa Tom hurt. "I'll meet this Mr. Alex. I'm not saying I'm going to tell him stuff, but I think your momma might need a little help with this one."

Jack wasn't sure what kind of help his mom might need, but he nodded. Grandpa Tom would handle it just fine for him. Jack went to bed twenty minutes later and slept soundly. Hopefully, Mr. Alex wouldn't mind meeting an old man.

~~~

Alex found himself watching for Jack. He didn't have any idea if he'd show or not, but he hoped so. Alex was still a little pissed at his dad because he wouldn't tell him about Heather, but he would get it soon enough. He was watching for his little baker too.

When Jack showed up with an older man with him, Alex stood up as they approached the table. He knew they were related by the eyes. No one but family could have eyes the color they had.

"Mr. Alex. This is my grandpa Tom. We…he wants to speak to you."

Alex stepped up to the counter and left his grandfather at the table. "Sir. Have a seat. I'm Alexander James." He put out his hand and was rewarded with a hard shake. "Your grandson is a very special young man."

"Thomas Laird. Yes, he is. Very special." They both looked over at the person in question. "He told me about the man who was stalking him yesterday. Did you know him?"

Alex let go of the breath he hadn't realized he'd been holding. "No, sir. Jack pointed him out as a joke, I think. But the man seemed to have an unhealthy interest in Jack. I watched for him as we went to the bus, but he didn't approach him."

Mr. Laird turned back to him with a smile. "Don't imagine too many men are stupid enough to approach you without an invite. You're a big man."

Alex flushed. "That I am. My father is as well. I only beat him by an inch. My mom is tall also."

"I wanted to thank you. Not many men would care about a kid enough to walk him to the bus stop. He and his momma are all I got. Well, that ain't true. I got my daughter, but there ain't a man in this here world that thinks she needs protecting."

Jack came back with his muffin, a cup of coffee, and a container of milk. His grandda took the coffee and Jack sat down with his muffin. He looked up at him.

"I'm sorry, Mr. Alex, can I get you something? I got about three bucks left." When Jack stood, Alex looked over at Mr. Laird and just caught the shake of his head. He was telling him not to offer to pay for whatever he wanted.

"Sure, I wouldn't mind one of those muffins. I have coffee, though. That's very nice of you." When Jack left to get the muffin, Alex turned to Mr. Laird. "I'm part owner here, sir. I don't need the boy to pay for my breakfast. I can well afford to pay for his as well as yours."

"Maybe I wasn't thinking of monetary just now but of pride. He has a great deal of it. His mother gave him that. You'd do well to remember that money doesn't mean squat to someone like Jack or my granddaughter."

Alex didn't understand, but he nodded. He didn't know the man's granddaughter.

They spoke for a bit longer and then Mr. Laird left. Jack finished his breakfast in much the same fashion as he had the day before. He cut up the muffin in to eight perfectly equal pieces and ate them without a single crumb falling on him or the tray.

"My mom works here," Jack said between bites. "She makes these for me at home. Not lately, the oven doesn't work anymore, but she does make these for Miss Caroline."

Alex felt the breath leave his body. He looked over at Lisa who was ringing out a customer and she winked at him when she saw him looking at her. He found himself hoping that she was his mother, but somehow knew that she wasn't.

"I'm not supposed to tell anyone who I am. It might...the welfare people might come back again or that woman. But she does okay, my mom, I mean. She works too hard, but we got each other." Alex looked at Jack as he continued to eat his breakfast. "She got hurt yesterday. I was wondering if I could ask you a question."

Alex nodded. He was going to ask him about why he'd hurt her, why he'd made her go to the hospital. Alex's mind was spinning out of control when he realized this child was hers.

"She said that somebody kissed her yesterday. And that he wanted to do it again." Jack played with the paper on his plate and didn't look up. "Why would someone kiss a girl? I mean, without having to do it. She said she didn't like it, but she said that she'd not been out for a long time so maybe…I don't know maybe she forgot how."

Alex didn't think she'd forgotten how. He started to say something else when he realized what else he'd said. "What do you mean she didn't like it? How could…what did she say about the kiss that she didn't like?"

"Gee, Mr. Alex, she just said she didn't like it. I don't know why anyone would do it in the first place. And tongues?" Jack shuddered. "That has got to be the grossest thing I've ever heard of."

Alex laughed. "You'll change your mind when you get older. What's your mom's name anyway?"

"Heather. Heather Laird. And she said the same thing to me."

Alex walked Jack to the bus stop again. Neither of them saw the man from yesterday, but they were both so lost in thought that Alex wasn't sure he'd see his mother if she walked right up to him. Heather, his Heather, had a son. A grown son, and she didn't want anyone to know about him. He decided to do a little research when he got back to his house.

Something wasn't right. Something he didn't understand was happening and he wanted answers. He called his mom on the way back to his house after leaving the bakery. He thought it best if he didn't see Heather Laird right now.

# Chapter 9

Heather hurt. Her arm hurt, her head hurt, even her hair hurt she was so tired. She was sure she was going to die soon and wondered if she would welcome it. She lifted the tray of six breakfasts over onto her shoulder and nearly cried out in pain. She was going to have to put it down again, but hoped she'd make it to the table first. Smiling as she went through the door, she was nearly in tears by the time she got there. She was putting the plate in front of the six businessmen when she heard the news behind her. Turning slowly, she looked at the screen.

"…total loss. There were no fatalities in this morning's blaze, but the place is a total loss. The Fire Chief is saying it looks like faulty wiring, but until further tests are made, they are marking it as suspicious."

When the camera pulled back, Heather dropped the plate in her hand. The air around her head seemed to be sucked away and she grabbed for the first thing she could touch. She felt someone push her down and before she knew it, she was sitting in a chair with her head between her knees.

"Deep breaths, miss. Take deep breaths. That's it. Come on now, don't faint on me. Deep breaths." She tried to sit up, but was shoved back down. "Not yet. You have to wait until I get my heart to beat properly first. Scared the shit outta me just now when I saw you falling."

"I'm okay now. I have to...please let me up. I'm fine now." She stood up and made the mistake of looking at the television again.

Her home. Her home was burning out of control. Blindly, she made her way to the door and out. She had to get there. She had to see if it really was true or some kind of cruel joke. She knew that it wasn't as she made her way to her block. She didn't even remember getting there only that she was there and watching along with several hundred other people as it burned.

She didn't know how long she stood there, but someone put something around her shoulders and was speaking to her. She looked at him and it took her several seconds to realize it was her grandda.

"Jack! Where's my baby? I have to find—"

"He's at school. I called, he's there. I spoke to him myself. One of the teachers, they're going to bring him to you. Said they'd be here soon. He's safe. We're all safe."

He held her while they watched the upper floors crumble down onto the lower ones. Then they watched as the whole structure came down. The police held everyone back as the fire department kept the building next to it under continuous spray.

Frozen water filled the street. Cars were covered in it, grimy now from the ash and soot. The air smelled of burned wood and plastic. Twisted pipes and other things, things that were so badly burned she could no longer tell what they were. They had lived there for eight years and now…now they had nothing.

"We'll be fine, love. You'll see. We'll be fine." Heather didn't realize she'd spoken out loud until he answered her, but she could tell by the look on his face that he knew they weren't going to be fine.

Jack arrived ten minutes later. He ran from the car he'd been brought in and leapt into her arms. She kept kissing him and holding him to her. She didn't want to think about what would have happened had he been home instead of school. He kept telling her he loved her and that he was happy to see her. She couldn't stop the tears from falling and felt them freeze on her cheeks.

The Red Cross showed up a few hours later. Heather was freezing by then and couldn't seem to get warm. She was trying to figure out where they were going to stay tonight when the offer of the shelter seemed their only hope. It was well after ten o'clock when she realized she'd have to find clean clothes to go to work.

Her grandda was arguing with her about it, but she told him that now they needed the money more than ever. She didn't want to leave them. She wanted to stay with them both and hold them until she felt better, but she knew that it was impractical and just a little insane. She needed to provide for them; she was all they had. She walked to the bakery and slipped into the back door.

Without speaking to anyone, Heather began pulling out the ingredients to make her first batch of cookies. She looked at the list in front of her, the one that had been left for her every day since she'd been working there, and began to divide up her tasks. As soon as she got the batter started, she would start the bread. After that, it would be the pies.

She heard someone come in and speak, but she didn't say anything to them. She wasn't sure what she might have said anyway. She just kept working. When she heard her name, she didn't turn around.

"If you need anything else today, I think I can get to it. I don't have anywhere to be right now." The small giggle escaped. "Boy, is that true."

"Heather, turn around and look at me, sweetheart." Caroline's voice was gentle, but she didn't turn. "I knew where you lived, but I didn't know it was your home until Lisa said you smelled of smoke. Did you lose everything?"

Not what was important, she wanted to say, but didn't. "Yes, ma'am. The entire building was a loss."

"Heather, honey, where will you stay now? Do you have family? Someone you can stay with?"

"I...I don't really want to talk about it right now, please. I have to get this done. I have to get finished because I have another job. I hope. I guess I might be fired." She just realized that she'd left without telling anyone. "I need to figure that out."

She heard him before she saw him. He was shouting her name so loud it felt as if he was in her head. When he whipped her around, she felt dizzy, but before she could get her bearings, he was crushing her to him. Alex.

He was saying something. She didn't think she'd heard him correctly so she pulled back and looked up at him. He repeated himself twice more before she pulled away from him.

"I said, where's Jack and your grandfather? Are they all right? The news said no one was hurt, but I couldn't be sure. Heather?"

She started backing away from him and bumped into the wall before she stopped. "How? How did you find them? Who told you about Jack?"

"You should have, but I found out on my own. I talked to them both this morning. Your son came here the other morning and then again today." His voice sounded harsh like he was pissed about something. "You didn't answer me, are they all right?"

"You have a son, Heather?" She looked over at Miss Caroline. "Is he with you or his dad?"

Heather looked at Alex. She knew in that moment that he knew about Jack's birth and his dad. She turned back to the table. "They're fine. He lives with me...me and my grandfather. He's...they're fine."

"Where are they? The news reporter said that all the people in the building were finding other places to live. Where are Jack and Mr. Laird?" She heard the coldness in his voice.

"The shelter on Fifth Avenue. They said we can stay there until we get back on our feet. I'm going to have to find another job soon. We won't be able to—"

"I'm going to go and get them and take them to my house. Do you need anything right now?" She shook her head and didn't say anything. "All right then."

She heard him leave, heard the front door bell jingle a happy tune when the door closed behind him. She started to knead the bread, but found she just didn't have it in her to try. They were going to be safe with him. Jack would be all right and he wouldn't have to live in the shelter. She waited until she thought Caroline was gone then looked around the kitchen.

She loved working here. She looked forward to coming to this job more than any of the others. She was going to miss it. She didn't have a coat, but she didn't think she'd need it so she slipped out the door she'd entered not so long ago and started walking. The only thought that kept her going was they were safe, Jack was safe.

~~~

Alex was sick to his stomach. The file still lay on his desk at home. He'd only just gotten off the phone with Heather's mom when the news came on. He glanced down at the familiar address before bolting out the door to find her. He'd searched everywhere and when his phone rang and it was Lisa telling him that Heather was at work, he saw red.

It hadn't occurred to him until he saw her that she might not have known about the fire until he could see that she'd been there; dirt and soot were on her clothes. He pulled up in front of the shelter when his phone rang. It was Wills.

"I don't have time to talk right now. Something has happened and I need to take care of it."

He heard her sigh. "Then you know. I'm so sorry, Alex. More than you know. He was such a wonderful man."

"Something happened to Mr. Laird? Oh shit, this is going to kill Heather. And Ja—"

"No. Who? Never mind. I was talking about Brick." Alex leaned against his car, trying to understand what she was talking about.

"What about Brick?" Alex nodded to the woman at the front desk, glad he'd called to have the Lairds ready and waiting. Both of them were waiting by the door.

"He's dead. It must have happened last night sometime. It was on the news..." Alex didn't hear anything else. Brick was dead? She must have made a mistake. Then he heard her shout his name.

"I'm here. Are you sure? I mean, what happened? Where at? Oh God, Amy. Is she all right?"

His first thought was Mik. He'd killed Brick for some reason. But Alex didn't want to contemplate that right now. He was opening the door for Jack when Wills spoke again.

"Amy is in the hospital. They'd been out, the two of them having dinner. When they got home, they must have startled a robber. The police are looking, but according to the six o'clock news, they have nothing as of yet."

Alex looked at Mr. Laird. He could see the curiosity on his face, along with sorrow and compassion. "I have to go, Wills. I want to make a few calls. If you hear anything, please let me know." He hung up and leaned heavily against his car.

"You friend?" Mr. Laird asked as he patted Alex on the back. Alex nodded. "I'm so sorry, son. Truly I am."

Alex drove on auto pilot going back to the bakery. He found that despite what he'd heard about Heather, he wanted to take her home and gather her in his arms and hold her. He wanted to keep her close.

"Mr. Alex, are you all right?"

Alex looked in the rear view mirror in the back seat at Jack. Again, he saw the same compassion he'd seen in the older man's eyes.

"I just found out a good friend of mine died. I was...we were partners in our own company until recently."

"I'm sorry, sir. Maybe you should take us back to the shelter. Mom will come back there and we can stay there." Jack patted him on the shoulder as he continued. "They don't care if we do. Maybe you don't need company right now."

Alex felt the tears well in his eyes. He couldn't speak for several moments because of the lump in his throat. Before he could form the words to answer the boy, Mr. Laird spoke.

"I think he might need the company, son. I know I did when I lost my Colleen." He turned in the seat and looked at the boy in the back. "Now there was a woman. Big, gray, soulful eyes that made a man think."

"Think about what, Grandpa Tom?"

Alex felt the laugh burst from his mouth as Jack's innocent question.

"'Bout kisses and long walks in the moonlight. 'Bout holding her hand and telling her that I love her."

Alex looked again in the mirror at Jack when he began making gagging noises. Alex was ready to pull over when he realized the kid wasn't sick, but making a comment on his grandda's wanting to be with a woman. He laughed again.

"You don't have a girlfriend, Jacky boy? Why, when I was your age, I had a dozen on each arm." The older man winked. "Time was I could have had my choice of women. All wanting to get a piece of your great grandda."

"Girls are weird," Jack groused. "Don't you think so, Mr. Alex?"

"They have their uses." He pulled up in front of the bakery as he answered. He slipped out of the car, asking the two of them to wait. Lisa was just locking up.

"Hey, Alex. Mom is in the back. She was cleaning up." He started back when she stopped him with her next statement. "She said Heather left."

"Left? Left where, when?" At her shrug, he went into the kitchen. "Caroline?" She'd been crying, he noticed. Her nose was red and her cheeks were blotchy. She looked as if she was upset or angry. Alex couldn't tell which.

"Please tell me she's with you. I don't know how to get in touch with her and I'm worried. She just left." Caroline continued to sob. "After you left, I came back to talk to her and she was simply gone. She didn't even have a coat."

"I'll find her." He was at once worried then furious with Heather. She'd upset his friend with her behavior. "I don't suppose you know if she has any friends? Someone she might have called?"

"She didn't have time for anyone. Not even herself." Alex turned to the doorway to see Mr. Laird and Jack. "She was working a lot to keep a roof over our heads."

# Chapter 10

Heather was freezing. And she ached. Not just her arm, though she could feel the pains shooting up her arm to her head like a jack hammer. Somewhere in her body she felt a coldness that seeped into her and started to fill her. She was sure it had nothing to do with the cold and more to do with what had happened. Twice she'd had to stop and rest and twice she'd fallen asleep standing up. She wasn't sure how much longer she could go on.

The all night diner was like a beacon to her. She went to it and its promise of warmth like a woman on a chocolate binge. She could barely open the door her hands were so cold. She ended up waiting until someone came out before she managed to slip inside. The heat was overwhelming at first and had her nearly go back out again. But someone was touching her, pulling her along until she was seated.

"...you hear me, Heather? Please, honey, answer me. Come on, you're scaring me."

Heather tuned to look at the person. It took her several seconds to realize who was speaking to her. Then a few more before she could focus on what was being said.

"Lisa...Miss Lisa? What are you doing here?" Heather looked around the tiny dining room. "Where are we?"

"The Trolley Café. I've called my mom. She's been so worried. We all have. She said for you to stay here until someone comes to get you." Lisa sounded so far away. Her voice was garbled and hard to understand. Heather looked at the cup someone put into her hands.

She couldn't hold it. It burned her fingers and felt too heavy in her hands. She wanted to sleep suddenly, curl up on the wide bench she was sitting on and go to sleep. But she needed to...something she needed to do. Then she realized Lisa was speaking again.

"...keep up your strength maybe. You need to get warm. You're a block of ice."

Heather doubted that ice felt like it was on fire much less tingle like she was. The shivering started then and she couldn't stop it. Her teeth banged hard together so many times they were beginning to hurt. When she thought about lifting a napkin from the table and stuffing it in her mouth to stop it, she closed her eyes against the pain when she'd lifted her arm. That was a mistake.

Her belly rolled and her head felt as if her neck didn't have the strength to hold up her head a minute longer. She felt herself sliding and rolling to the floor. The cool tile hurt her skin, but she couldn't move her mouth to speak. Her eyes wouldn't stay open.

As she drifted out, everything fading, she let the blackness take her away. She heard a voice then, loud, demanding, and male. It was the hard timbre of Alex.

Heather woke slowly, degree by degree coming awake as though she'd been asleep for days. She didn't open her eyes for a long while—just felt, listened, and absorbed.

It was quiet. Very quiet, actually. She could hear a soft creak, a sigh of something giving in protest. There was music; this too was soft and she thought it was something classical, but couldn't be sure. A whisper of sound was far away, or so it seemed to her.

There was light in her room. Almost bright, but she wasn't entirely sure with her eyes closed. She didn't remember leaving a light on, but she'd been so tired lately there would be no telling what she'd do to get to sleep. Something had...when the pain pierced her head, she moved away from the thought that was just there then gone.

Things smelled floral, almost too sweet. She didn't have time for flowers, or money for that matter, but she thought that's what she smelled. The scented thingy she'd had in her room was very nice, she finally thought, and decided to remember the brand to purchase again. She frowned when she rolled to her side. She opened her eyes to see what she was caught on.

It came crashing back on her like a live wire racing along her mind. The fire, the burn, the finality of it all.

She had no home and she didn't know where her son was. She started to sit up when a voice from the corner made her jerk around. She couldn't stop the moan of pain or the spill of tears.

"Shhhh. Everyone is all right. Shhhh, now, you're safe." Heather heard the soft murmured words and the soft, comforting tone of the voice.

"Jack? My son?" Heather couldn't swallow, much less talk very well. Her body ached and her throat felt as if acid had been poured down it.

"They're fine. Alex took them to his house. He only...Alex just went home to check on them." The voice moved closer; the woman spoke again. "They've been so worried about you."

Hospital. She was in a hospital room and there was an IV in her hand. Heather looked around the bright walls and polished wood. The television was flashing pictures of flowers and animals across it as music sounded from it. She looked at the woman with her.

"Who?" Her throat ached to speak. She wanted a drink in the worst way. "Who are you?"

"Candace James, I'm Alexander's mother. We met the other day." Candace sat on the bed. "We sort of met the other day at my house. Alex had brought you there after you were burned. My husband, Edgar, took you back to the bakery."

Heather closed her eyes at the memory. Alex had kissed her and taken her to—"I need to go."

Candace laughed. "Alexander said you were stubborn. I don't think you have the strength just yet for that, dear. You were close to hypothermia by the time they got you here. I don't know what made you run around like that without proper attire, but you should know better. Alexander has been worried sick."

Heather doubted that, but said nothing. She remembered walking. It had been cold and the fight…he knew now and she didn't want to be around when he started asking questions. And he would too.

"I lost my job. I need to find another one." She found that her throat hurt less now that she was using it. "I can't afford this."

Heather noticed that the flowers on the table were violets. She loved the tiny purple and white flowers and wondered who they belonged to. She closed her eyes, exhausted.

"I'm sure arrangements can be made about your bill," Mrs. James said, breaking though her haze. "But for now, you must rest. Alexander will be glad to know you're awake. He wanted to speak to you."

Heather was sure he would. Though why he was concerned was beyond her. She nodded to the older woman and closed her eyes. She couldn't stop the tears that fell and wasn't really sure who or what they were for. Herself or Jack.

When she woke the next time, it was dark. She didn't need to open her eyes to know that she was alone in the room this time. The room didn't have the small sounds that it had before, the sounds of the rocker Mrs. James had been in, the sounds she knew now were the whisper of crepe-soled shoes over tiled floor.

She was alone, she figured, in every since of the word. The welfare people would come now and take Jack from her. Without a job, house, or any prospects of getting any of them for a while, she knew that they would find her unfit. Her mother had turned her in to them so many times over the years that Heather couldn't begin to count them. Now that she had mounting hospital bills and no way to pay them…well, she wasn't sure what to do now. It seemed her mother was finally going to get her wish.

Then there was Mr. James, Alexander. He'd want answers. Though she still hadn't figured out why he cared. He didn't like her overly much, she thought. She wondered fleetingly if he'd talked to her mother and knew that he had. He wouldn't be the type of man to leave anything to chance if he wanted to have sex with someone.

She wasn't stupid. She knew that he wanted her. Why, she didn't know, but he did. She was completely out of his league. He was rich and had everything while she wasn't and didn't. She had less than nothing. She was in the hole as far as she could see.

She rolled to her side and looked at the pretty flowers again. She knew little to absolutely nothing about men. They baffled her more than her math homework ever had. Why someone as beautiful as Mr. James would want her was insane.

He was beautiful too. Dark golden hair that was just a little too long in the back. It curled just enough to give him an appealing unkempt look. He was tall too, towering over her by nearly eight inches. His face was all angles and lines, hard jaw, masculine nose that reminded her of the painting she'd seen in the museum when she and Jack had gone on one of their free days.

Mr. James…Alex, his mouth looked hard and his lips seemed almost too full for a man, but sexy at the same time. When he'd brushed them over hers or kissed them along her skin, she felt needed, sexy, and very needy.

His hands fascinated her. They were large like he was, yet tender on her body. His long fingers had plucked at her nipples and heated her skin with their touch, bringing her to a fevered pitch. Sighing, she rolled to her back and looked up to see the man she'd just been thinking about.

~~~

Alex thought she was asleep, she'd been so still. He had hoped to see her awake and now that she was, he didn't have a clue what to say to her. He let the door go so that it would drift quietly closed before he spoke.

"I didn't think you were awake. I hope I didn't wake you up." He felt stupid. "I wanted to come by and see you."

"No." Her answer sounded husky and Alex felt his body respond.

"Mom said you woke when she was here yesterday morning. I've been out of town." He wondered what he was saying then decided to stick to what he wanted from here on before he made a bigger fool of himself. "Your family is safe. I have them at my house. Jack hasn't been to school the last few days until today. I made sure they were aware of your circumstances."

"You mean that we're homeless? I'm sure they were glad to know that bit of information," she snapped at him.

He could hear the bitterness in her voice. He would have to be stupid or deaf not to. For some reason, that pissed him off.

"No, I told them you were ill and that until arrangements could be made between you and I, they would be staying with me. I didn't tell them anything more than that."

She looked at him sharply. "Arrangements? What sort of...you'll hold my family hostage until I sleep with you? Then what happens after you're finished? We're back on the streets? Well that sounds just like every man I know."

He staggered back. He couldn't believe she thought so little of him or of herself for that matter. To think he'd only kept them safe to blackmail her into...sex?

"Is that what you think, Heather? That I'm the type of man who would hold a child and an old man just so I can fuck you?" She flinched. "That's right. That's what you think, isn't it?"

"You're a man, aren't you? Don't men, all men, want to fuck someone even if it has nothing to do with sex?"

Alex thought about what her mother had told him about her and her stepfather. "Is that what Baxter wanted.

Did he want to fuck you too and when he got what he wanted, you told on him?"

Alex knew the moment the words were out of his mouth they weren't true. He was ready to tell her how sorry he was, that he hadn't meant them, that he was angry when the door behind him burst open. A small streak flew across the room and was in her bed before Alex realized what or who it was. It wasn't until Mr. Laird, Tom as he'd asked Alex to call him, patted him on the back that he realized that the small missile was Jack.

"Looks good, don't she?" Tom asked as he skirted around the chair. "How you feeling, girl? Scared us, you did."

Alex watched her with her son. She loved him, that much was evident. He could see his mom doing the same, holding back her aches and pains to love on him or Wills. Heather soothed her son when he asked why she was crying by explaining how she was so happy to see him. Alex could see the pain in her eyes and not from being ill, but the pain of what he'd said. He glanced over at Tom when he felt the man staring at him. Alex knew he could see the pain too.

Alex knew that Tom may not know what they'd been fighting about, but he knew that his granddaughter was in pain. Alex tried not to squirm under the man's gaze, but he was uncomfortable. It wasn't until he looked away that Alex let out the breath he'd been holding.

The visit was short. The nurse brought a tray of clear liquids in for Heather and Alex was sure she'd only eaten what she did because Jack had badgered her into it. She was drifting off when the three of them left the room. They were to the elevator when Tom turned back to him.

"You gonna fix this?"

Alex didn't even try to pretend he didn't know what he was talking about. "Yes, sir. If she'll let me. I said something…I told her—"

"Don't rightly care what you said, young man, but I want it fixed." They both looked at Jack standing so still in front of them. "She'll kill for him, but for herself…well, she'd about do anything for him."

With that, he stepped on the yawning elevator and pushed the button. With a final "fix it" as the doors closed, Alex was left standing there alone. He made his way back to her room. He felt like a man going to his own hanging standing outside her door. He hadn't meant to say those things, wasn't even sure he believed them anymore. He hated himself that he had said them and hated himself even more that he'd hurt her.

When he entered her room again, he had decided to tell her he was sorry and offer to put them all up in an apartment and pay the rent until she found it in her heart to forgive him.

He expected her to be hurt when he went back inside. He even expected tears. He hated them, but felt he deserved them from her. He didn't know what had happened between her and Steven Baxter, but he was sure as he was standing there it wasn't the way her mother had told him it had been. What he didn't expect was her to have a bargain of her own to offer.

"I'll let you fuck me as much as you want if you let my family stay until I can…until I can get us back on our feet."

# Chapter 11

Edgar looked over at his wife before slanting his eyes back to his son. He wasn't sure what Alex wanted them to say so he waited before speaking. He honestly was hoping for them to tell him it was a joke, but was reasonably sure it wasn't. He decided to come at this from another angle.

"Did you believe her when she explained about Baxter?" He knew the moment he'd asked that he wasn't going to like the answer. "You didn't ask her, did you?"

"No. I didn't...she was so upset before that I thought I'd not bring it up again. Then she throws this at me."

Alex got up to pace. Edgar moved closer to his wife. Candace had told him that she'd liked the girl. She said that she was as stubborn as Alex and had thought that the two of them would suit. Suit what he wasn't sure, but he let it go...for now.

"Alexander, there are more than just the two of you involved in this. There's that young boy to think of." Candace frowned when Alex said nothing to her. "Alexander, are you listening to me?"

"Yes. You don't think I've thought about her son? I like that kid. He's smart, friendly, and loves her to death.

But I didn't make the offer to her, she told me. She said she's only doing this for him. If it were...Christ." Alex paced some more. "If she didn't have him or the old man, she'd probably...fuck. Now what the hell am I supposed to do?"

No one said anything about his language. His mother hated that word and he knew she wasn't overly fond of the situation either. But he was a grown man. Edgar looked over at his daughter and her husband for help.

"Are you in love with her, Alex? This girl, do you love her?"

Edgar smiled at Jared.

"No. I don't...I'm not going to be either." When Jared snorted, Alex turned on him. "It's not the same as you and Wills. I will never give my heart to another woman for her to trample into the dirt."

"Sometimes it's not a matter of giving it away, Alex, as it is someone earning it." Edgar took the look his son gave him for saying it, but he couldn't help it. He felt his son's pain like it was his own. Alex's ex-wife, Bethany Sheppard, had hurt him. And it wasn't until years later that they'd, his mother and he, had gotten the whole story.

Bethany had been from a good family. In fact, the two families had been nearly in each other's pockets since the adults had met before they'd had children. Bethany was the older of the children. Then Alex and Charles, Bethany's brother, then Wills. The children had played together all their lives.

Then one summer, Bethany announced she was in love with Alex. Alex had just turned nineteen and Bethany had been three years older. She'd told them all, including Alex, that they'd be married the following summer. Everyone was deliriously happy for them.

Alex was in love. Any fool could see it. His mother had commented on it almost daily how happy he looked. But she didn't think it was the smartest of moves that they wed. At least so young, she'd told them.

Alex and she had fought and the closer the wedding came, the more depressed Candace became. She had tried to talk to him, tried to convince him to wait, but the more she tried, the harder he dug in. It wasn't two weeks after the wedding that he'd come home upset and needing to talk to them.

"Bethany is pregnant," he'd told them. "And it's...I'm not the father. She knew this before we married."

Candace didn't say anything as she held their son. She simply held him as he poured the entire story out.

"She was sick on our honeymoon. Every day. I kept asking her what was wrong and she said it was the flight, or the different food. I believed her. I was a fool."

"You weren't a fool," his mother said. "You were in love. I'm so sorry, baby. I know this hurts."

"Are you sure it's not yours?" They both looked at him when he'd asked. "I'm sure you didn't remain celibate before you were married, did you?"

"No, sir, but... Well, I used protection when we had sex. I didn't...kids are not in the picture right now. I'm trying to get this business going with Brick and we...I didn't want a baby just yet. I thought she understood."

They fought, Bethany and Alex, bitterly and long. When years later Alex had told them, long after the accident, neither he nor Candace could believe it. Bethany wanted to continue on with her affairs and she could see no reason for Alex to be upset about it. Then the accident.

Charles and Bethany had been driving back from the airport after dropping off their parents. Bethany was about six months then, her belly rounded and full. Charles was just to turn sixteen in a few weeks. He had been driving.

The police said that his inexperience had caused the accident. He'd over compensated when he'd hit a slick spot on the wet road. The car, a compact, had hit the guardrail several times before it had stalled in the road only to be hit broadside by an oncoming tractor trailer. Charles was killed instantly, his neck broken, as was most of his body. Bethany had been alive when they reached the hospital, but the baby had been lost. But it was the last thing she'd said to Alex that had hurt him, killed something inside of him that day.

"You were nothing to me," she'd said. "Nothing but a means to an end and even in that you failed me. I never loved you, never liked you most of them time. I'm glad the child wasn't yours."

There had been more, more biting remarks, more recriminations, and more of her telling him what a failure he'd been. And he'd taken it all from her, taken every word she'd uttered. When they'd wheeled her to surgery, Alex left the hospital.

It was several hours before they found him to tell him she was dead. A hemorrhage that they'd not found until it was too late had caused internal bleeding and she was simply gone.

The Sheppards had wanted to blame Alex, but they couldn't with him not even in the car. And it wasn't until the funeral that they'd found out that her parents knew about the child and that Alex wasn't the father. They had not spoken to them since.

Edgar watched his son pace and wondered if this woman, this baker, could be the one to make him love again. He wanted to talk with the girl, and her son, and see their worth.

"Did she give you a reason for her...offer, I guess? What did she say when you asked her about it?" Wills, ever practical.

"She said that she knew I'd talked to her mother and that since I'd come to my own conclusions about her, she might as well take advantage of it. And before you ask, yes, I did talk to her."

When he didn't continue, Edgar looked at him. "And?"

"And...and...I'm not sure. I think I believe her. I mean, all the things point to what she's saying, but I just don't know."

"Oh for heaven's sake, Alexander, what things? What is this woman saying about her own daughter?"

Alex sat down before answering his mom. "That Heather seduced her step-father into her bed and got pregnant to break up their marriage."

~~~

Mik looked at the pictures before him. They showed Alexander James with a kid. He didn't have any idea who the kid was, nor did he give a tinker's damn, but he filed away the information for use later. He wanted Alexander.

Brick had been useful, but not what Mik had wanted. When he had perused the company to help him with his "problem," he'd wanted them both. What he'd gotten was the brawn not the brain. Brick had been good, just not good enough. So Mik had had to let him go.

He smiled when he'd thought of the man and his wife. So stupid and so very trusting. Mik hadn't wanted to hurt the woman, but sometimes one had to go the extra mile in order to get better results.

"What do we know of Alexander now? Is he ready to open another company? Or is he still trying to be retired?" Mik looked up at his man when he didn't answer right away. "Well?"

"He's bought himself into a bakery—House of Aromas. He and his new partner have started on the renovations into the building already. He has some property, a house that he's also having some work done on."

"But? What are you not telling me? I know there has to be something along the lines of computer somewhere. The man is just too good not to want to play some." Mik wanted him to open another company, something he could get into. Something, Mik hoped, he could use against the man.

"Nothing so far. I have been watching him at the coffee shop, keeping an eye on what he's into there. He has a good security system on his Internet access so it's taking me awhile to break into his computer, but I will." David was his best computer expert and if he was having issues, he knew it had to be good. But there was more.

"Are you going to tell me what else or do I need to keep guessing? If I have to keep guessing…" Mik pulled out his gun and laid it on the desk. "I'm going to start shooting something. Or…someone."

David pulled at his collar. He was sweating now, Mik could see, and sweating a great deal.

"I think I may have been made. Mr. James, he saw me. Him and that brat, they saw me hanging around the bakery. Then there was…I'm sure they saw me snapping the pictures of him."

Mik picked up the gun and fired. David was dead before he hit the floor. Mik looked at the two men at the door. Neither of them turned around when the shot had been fired and he smiled at that. No one would say a word either. He knew as well as they did that he'd kill them if they did.

"You, by the door. What's your name?" He needed a replacement and it was as good a time as any to get one.

"Jimmy Dugan, sir. And this here is Danny Dugan, my brother." The man looked over at his brother. "We can…you want so we can get rid of the body for you?"

*Ah*, Mik thought, *an intellect.* "Yes. Then I need you to go and see what you can find out about Alexander James and the brat. I want everything you can find including if there are any women in his life. Don't disappoint me or you'll find yourself in the same place David here is."

Both men looked down at the dead man and shuddered. Good, that's what he wanted, fear and a little terror. He wanted them to get him what he wanted.

Alexander was the man to get. Mik had known this the moment he'd realized that breaking into banks with a computer instead of a gun was safer. He'd been building his clientele for months as he watched the A&B Company grow and expand. And he'd been planning. The small glitches had been planned right down to the irregularity of them. First the system would be down for a matter of seconds, then more. He'd just started to make them be offline for more than ten minutes when his geek had died of a massive stroke.

Mik had been looking for someone to get him into the system and Alexander James was his man. He already had the perfect plan figured out on how to make him work for him and do what he'd wanted. And his lovely sister would make a nice addition to his little harem of broken women.

# Chapter 12

Heather was going home. Well, not home, but to Mr. James' house. She'd not seen him since she'd told him she'd sleep with him. But he had called her twice. Each call had ended with her in tears and him pissed off. She didn't know what he was so mad about. He wasn't doing anything more than lending them money until she could get them out.

She watched her grandda as he sat in the big chair waiting on the doctor to come in to release her. She'd been waiting for over an hour and hoped that they could get going soon. Heather was still trying to figure out if she should tell her grandda what she was doing or just keep it a secret.

"It's going to be nice having you there with us, kiddo. I've missed you and I know that Jack has. He can't seem to settle down much without you." She missed them both too. "Jack wanted to stay home today, but he had that test. And yeah, I've been studying with him."

"I didn't say anything." She took a deep breath before she continued. "Grandda, there's something you should know. It's about Mr. James and me. We…that is to say, he and I are —"

"Hello, Miss Laird," the doctor said as he entered the room after a brisk knock. "I guess you want to go home today, right? That's good. Very good. Now I don't want you going back to work right away. You'll need to keep rested so there is no relapse."

She didn't answer and she didn't look at her grandda either. She was going back to work as soon as she could find a job and since Caroline had called her and told her she could come back there — of course with a permission slip from the doctor — she had that job as well. Her arrangement with Mr. James notwithstanding. She was going to get out of this as quickly as possible.

"And now…Mr. Laird, I was wondering if you might step out for a moment? I'd like a word or two with your granddaughter, please. You understand." The doctor, Fredrick Sams, shook her grandda's hand as he left. "Now, there are some things that you wanted to discuss?"

Heather had spoken to the nurse yesterday about getting on the birth control pill. She'd also asked the nurse about making sure she'd never get pregnant, again but the nurse had told her that they didn't do that to single women unless there was a medical issue that required it.

"I want to get on some sort of birth control. I don't…I can get the prescription at the clinic, but I want to make sure I get something really strong." She felt her face heat up. "I have a child and I've no wish for anymore."

He looked at her for several seconds. "Shelly told me that you wanted to have a tubal ligation. I try to recommend that single women, especially single women as young as you are, Miss Laird, not to do something that may not be reversed later. You may change your mind and your husband will be upset with you for doing something so drastic."

She didn't point out that it was her body and that the chances of her getting married, much less having another child, were slim to none. She just nodded. "Yes, she told me. I still want to get on the pill, please. Can you write me something up for that?" She didn't know anything about this sort of thing, only what she'd read in the pamphlet that she'd been given last night.

"Of course. But you will need to take precautions before you depend on this method to prevent you from conceiving. I would recommend at least an entire cycle. Two if possible."

Heather didn't plan on ever taking just the pill to keep her from getting pregnant. She was planning on Mr. James taking his own necessary steps to prevent a child.

With her prescription in hand, she and her grandda left the hospital. The taxi ride was exhausting, but worth it. Grandda had told her that Mr. James was out of town until tomorrow night.

"Don't think he thought you'd be getting out before a few more days. He's going to be a bit disappointed that you got sprung early." Heather doubted that unless it was because he wasn't going to get his first payment. "But he'll be back. Had a friend of his pass. Heard him tell his momma that he and this Brick feller were close as brothers."

Heather knew he'd gone to Cincinnati, but didn't know why. She didn't think that they would be on a personal level anytime soon, if ever. He didn't like her anymore than she liked him. This was just a means for them both to get what they wanted. She just hoped that when they left, and leave they would, that Jack wouldn't be too upset with her.

She leaned her head back against the seat and closed her eyes. She had planned it out to the letter, this arrangement with him. She would have sex with him whenever he wanted to and she would save her money. She figured it wouldn't take any more than two months to save enough money to put a deposit on another apartment. Sometime after the new year, she thought.

She had called her other landlord and he said that she wasn't getting her deposit back because there wasn't any place for him to look over. He'd thought it was funny that because of a fire, he was getting to keep all the tenants deposits.

By the time they pulled up in front of the house, she felt like she'd been run over several times and left for dead. But when she got in the house, she nearly wept. She didn't have a clue where she was supposed to sleep. Her grandda took her to the second floor.

"I called Alex last night to tell him you sweet talked the doc into letting you go. He said I was to make sure you were put into his room."

He'd spoken so quietly that she turned to look at him. "I'm sorry, Grandda. But I needed—"

"I don't know what you're doing, girl. I don't think I wanna either. You sleeping with this man, it's your business, yours and his. But if I find out you...you'd better not be doing something I'll be ashamed of, girl."

She lowered her head. She was ashamed. More ashamed in that moment than when she'd gotten pregnant.

"It's not what you think. You don't…it's not what you think." He lifted her chin and looked at her. "It's not. Please, just let it go."

He stared at her for several seconds longer. She felt as if he was looking deep into her soul. Heather knew there were tears falling, she could feel them as they spilled over her cheeks, but she didn't move to wipe them. She let him look his fill.

"I see. Yeah, I see." He moved away then turned back to her. "You do what you have to do and I'll do the same. I don't want Jacky-boy to know about this, you hear?"

"Yes. Grandda, I'm—"

"Don't. I don't think…just don't. I'll be going out for a bit. Will you be all right? I'll pick up Jack on the way back through."

"Yes, sir. Thank you for Jack." He didn't even turn back to her, just nodded and when down the stairs.

Heather turned back and looked at the room that Mr. James had sent her to. He'd done this on purpose. Made it clear to the man she loved that she belonged to Alex James. She was his whore. Without thought as to how pissed the master of the house would be, Heather moved down the stairs and to the opposite end of the house where Grandda had told her he and Jack had rooms.

She found a small room just off the kitchen. It looked as though it might be a servant's room. Thinking it suited not only her position in the house, but also her status as a person, Heather crawled into the bed and cried herself to sleep.

~~~

Alex was exhausted. The trip to Cincinnati and back in one day had taken its toll on him. Then there was the added stress of going through Brick's things at the office.

Amy had told him that he could take it all, even the things he had at the house. Even, she said, the things he had hidden in their mattress.

"He was afraid, Alex. He kept telling me that he should have listened to you, should have known that after all these years you were the smarter of the two of them."

Alex didn't say anything. He hadn't known what to say to a grieving widow of his best friend. He held her hand until she stopped crying then went to their room and gathered the files and disks that were under their mattress. He then went to the office.

Alex knew there were safes in the building, safes that only he and Brick had known about. Mostly they had used them as fire safes, back-ups of files, payroll, and accounts. On occasion, they would put payments in there, checks that they'd get over the weekends when neither of them had the time to go to the banks. It had also been used to hide the bottle of scotch. The one they had said they would share when they were fifty and rich as Midas.

At first glance, it looked as if Brick's office had been tossed. But Alex, knowing his friend, knew it was just the way he'd left it the last time he'd been in. The man had no sense of tidiness in his office. Alex stepped over a shoe and several wadded up balls of paper on his way across the room. Sitting behind the desk, he looked around the room.

It was a mess and other than the things strewn across the floor, if one looked hard enough, they could see that there was a method to his clutter. It only took Alex two minutes to find what he knew was there.

The pictures on the desk had been sorted. Rather than the plethora of pictures of his wife and parents, there was now a single photo of him. Alex picked up the picture and looked at it.

He and Brick had gone to Italy a few years back. The shot was of him toasting the wine they'd been drinking. Alex smiled at the memory. They'd had a good time together. And Brick had met Amy.

He didn't bother opening the frame. He simply put it into his coat pocket and went out again. He met no one either on his way in or his way out. Going to his old office, he went directly to the office safe and pulled out everything that was there then left again.

Now he was home. The silence of the house was the first thing he noticed. He thought that Tom would be there with Heather. When he'd called him to tell him that she was being released, Alex had made the decision to come back. Now he didn't know what to do with her.

He went up to his bedroom to see her and found the room, like the rest of the house, empty. Going down to the lower level, he saw her going across the living room toward the kitchen. She stopped when she saw him. He nearly burst out laughing when she raised her chin at him.

"Heather. Tom was supposed to tell you where my bedroom is. Maybe you changed your mind." A large part of him hoped that she had, but even more of him hoped that she hadn't.

"He did. And if you don't mind, I'll take the room down off the kitchen." She crossed her arms over her chest as she continued. "I said I'd have sex with you, not sleep with you."

He wanted her. He wanted her with a desperation that he'd never felt before. The clock in the hall chimed eleven times. Alex moved down the stairs toward her.

"It seems that we have plenty of time to get some things squared away between us. You said that I was to provide you with protection. I've done that. You'll find condoms in my room, next to the bed."

She stiffened when he was a foot from her. She didn't back away, but he could see the strain of the need to do so in her eyes. He wanted to taste her, he found. He wanted to taste every part of her before he buried himself deep inside of her. Reaching out to her, he ran his knuckles down her soft cheek.

"It's...its daylight out. You can't mean to...you don't want this now." Her breath was warm against his hand.

"Oh, but I do."

Cupping his hand at the back of her neck, he pulled her forward. She resisted slightly, he didn't expect anything less, but she didn't fight him. When her mouth was only a breath away, he felt her hands touch his waist and he groaned. If a simple touch from her could make him feel like this, he wondered what her body would feel like beneath him.

The first brush of his mouth over hers sent his heart pounding. When he nipped at her lower lip, brought it into his mouth, and suckled it, he felt his cock lengthen and harden more. He felt her tremble when he pulled her close to him, felt her pulse pound in her breast even as he pulled her hips to his.

Time had no meaning. The colors of the room, bright in the day, seemed to swirl around them. Sounds receded until all he could hear was her breathing hard and his own blood roaring through his head. Need, a living, breathing thing, was coiled tight inside of him and he wanted to let it go.

Lifting her up by his hands at her ass, she wrapped her legs around him. Turning, Alex started back up the stairs. He had to stop twice, once to suckle at her neck, the second because he was sure they weren't going to make it and the stairs would have to do. By the time they got to his bedroom, her blouse was off and her bra pushed up over her full breasts. Alex had his pants undone and his cock strained to be released from his boxers.

When he laid her on the bed, her legs still tight around him, he took her nipple into his mouth and nipped at it. Heather arched up off the bed, her back bowing up as he sucked hard on the tip.

"Please. Please, I need you." He wanted her as well. Moving off her, he nearly whimpered himself when he pulled away.

"Take off your pants. Hurry. I need to be inside of you right now." As she did what he asked, he stood and took off his jeans. His shirt was almost off when he looked down at her bare body.

Christ, she was perfect. Her rosy nipples were peaked hard against large, full breasts. The flush of her skin, dewy with her need, sparkled and shown in the morning sunlight that made his mouth water. Her tiny waist and the flare of her hips made him hungry, hungrier than he'd ever been for a woman, but it was her face that held him. The darkness of her eyes, the blue nearly black, the pink of her cheeks and her swollen lips made him want more, need more than just her body. It also made him take a step back. Then another and another until he was several feet from the bed. Before either of them could say a word, he snatched up his pants and left the room.

# Chapter 13

Jimmy watched the man leave the house. He'd been watching this house for three days now and this was the first time he or his brother had seen the man they'd been sent to find. Jimmy thought it was sort of stupid. The man was right where they'd thought he'd be, at home. But now, he was off again.

Glancing down at his notes, he wondered if he should tell Mr. Black about the old man and the boy. He'd seen a taxi come and go a few hours ago, but had been taking a leak and had missed if anyone had gotten out or into the thing. By the time he'd gotten his zipper up, the thing was pulling away. Then about twenty minutes later, the old man had left again. He'd figured the house was empty until about an hour ago.

He couldn't begin to figure out rich people. So far as he was concerned, they were all nuts. Take Mr. Black. He had tons of stuff, big televisions, food in that big old house of his, but he seemed to always be looking for a way to get more. Jimmy looked over at his brother who was sleeping in the black SUV until his turn to watch for Mr. James.

They had nothing. Less than nothing, to be truthful. But they had a job, and sometimes, if they was real careful, they could go out with a pretty girl. 'Course she had to be paid, and that's why they didn't do it much, but still it was enough for them.

He needed to follow this character James and he walked over to the car to get going. Jimmy started it up, did a u-turn, and followed. It never occurred to him that this James dude would know he was being followed and to take care. Jimmy thought everyone was too trusting and didn't think this guy was any different. His cell phone rang as he was coming up behind the other man's car at a light.

"Have you found our friend yet?" Mr. Black said in way of greeting.

"Didn't know he was a friend, sir. Should I maybe tell him you wanna talk to him? Me and my brother, we've been doing it stealth like for the past few days. If he's your friend, well, we co…"

"He's not my friend you fuck-tard. It's just an expression," Mr. Black snarled at him. Jimmy had a second of hot temper hit his system then he calmed as his boss continued. "Where the fuck is he? And I swear to Christ I will come up there and shoot you if you tell me you don't know."

"He's in the car in front of me. Got himself a big monster so it's easy to follow. Don't know where he's headed just yet, but he is going there." Jimmy looked over at his brother as he stirred. "He ain't been at his house for a few days, just got back today. He ain't got no security in yet, but there is some people working on the house. Construction guys."

"There was a boy with him. Do you see him? Is he with our target?" Jimmy tried to see if the kid was in the car, but he was sure he was in school, so that's what he told Black.

"Nah, he ain't. The old man, he took him off to the school first thing. That kid goes to a fancy school for the gifted. They got them some tight security there." Jimmy turned down the street when his "target" did. "He's going to the mall. Can't stand that place. Want I should wait in my car next to his or go in with him?"

Jimmy wanted to laugh at the man's string of curse words. But wisely, he kept his laughter to himself and his mouth closed. This man had a wicked temper and Jimmy thought that even the two hundred or so miles wasn't far enough away for him to get shot. So he waited.

"I want you to report to me every day where he goes, who he meets, and how long he's there. I want you to do this precisely and without any issues. Do I make myself clear?" Jimmy grinned at Mr. Black. "I'm paying you to keep an eye on him, and if he goes into the mall, then you fucking better be in there right behind him."

After closing the phone, Jimmy left the car and entered the mall. It was a big place, Jimmy discovered, and it was looking like Christmas had done comed early.

The place was a three-level building with more shops in it than all of his home town of Shelbyville had all over it. And the smell of the restaurant was enough to make a body wish he hadn't skipped his breakfast. It took him five minutes of wandering around before he found Mr. James. The man was in one of those nice, posh woman's places. Grabbing himself a Danish and a coffee, Jimmy found a chair and sat down to wait.

~~~

Jack watched for his ride home. School had let out about ten minutes ago, but he wasn't worried. He knew his grandpa Tom or Mr. Alex would be by soon. Jack wanted to get home; he knew that his mom was going to be there when he got there.

The house wasn't really his home. He knew it was just a stopping place until his mom could find them another one. But he liked it. Mr. Alex had a pool and lots of room. The big television with cable had been fun at first, but Jack hadn't ever watched all that much television before the fire and saw no reason to do so now. Then there were the guys from Stone Construction.

There were all sorts of things being done to the house. Jack thought that the rooms they were tearing down looked just fine before they started hacking at them, but didn't comment. Sometimes adults terrified him. They didn't like kids and especially ones that had no father and were poor.

He'd watched a man called Jared and another called Conley for hours over the weekend. Jack didn't think they knew he was there so he sat quietly and tried to figure out what it was they were doing. When another big piece of white board came in the room, he watched as they set it against the wall and screwed it up. The drill had screamed out a noise as it set the screws. When Conley had turned to him, it was all Jack could do not to cringe.

"You want to make a few bucks, kid?" Jack turned around to see who he might be speaking to. "You, I'm talking to you. You want to earn some pocket money?"

Jack stood up. "Yes, sir. No, sir. I mean…I can help you if you need me. But you don't have to pay me. I'm just, I like watching what you're doing."

"Yeah, we saw that. I need you to go down to the truck, the big green one with the silver tool box in the back. There's a big box of screws on the lip. Here." He handed Jack one of the screws from his apron. "This is the size we need. Got it?"

Jack nodded and took off. He was racing out the door when Mr. Alex came inside. He paused only long enough to tell him he was going to the truck. Mr. Alex told him to put his coat on. Laughing, Jack had found the boxes of screws, measured the ones in the box with the one he had, and hoped that he got the right one. He took the box up and was rewarded with an apron like they had on and a chance to use the screwdriver. Jack had been in heaven. He'd stayed out of the way as best he could and had asked only a few of the questions that had been burning through his head.

By then end of the day, he had ten dollars in his pocket and a promise of more next weekend if he wanted the job. That was still two days away and Jack couldn't wait. His grandpa Tom walked up and sat down next to him.

"Your momma is home. She looks good." Grandpa Tom made no effort to get up and catch the bus home so Jack waited. "She's gonna be a little tired for a bit so you don't go badgering her for a couple of days."

"Yes, sir." Jack didn't know what that meant, but had a good idea. "Will we be moving soon, you think?"

Grandpa Tom looked out at the buses pulling away from the school. "Don't think so. I wanted to have a talk with you, son. Man to man, all right?"

"Yes, sir." Jack didn't like the sound of his voice, but he didn't say anything. When he reached out and took Jack's hand, he knew something was wrong.

"First, I wanna tell you that your momma loves you. You know that, don't you?" Jack nodded. "Well...if you know that then you know that she'd do anything for you. Anything. What she does now, it ain't bad, it's..."

Their bus pulled up and they both stood to get on it. Jack had his student pass and Grandpa Tom had his senior card. The two of them took a seat about halfway back and settled in. The ride would take about twenty minutes.

His mom had been honest with him. He knew who his father was. He also knew the man was his step grandfather. Jack also knew that he wasn't supposed to know how he'd been conceived. But he'd heard his mom tell Vickie that he'd raped her that Steven had tied her to the bed after he'd drugged her and took her. He wasn't quite clear on the taking part, but he knew it had to do with sex.

Jack looked up at his grandpa Tom and wondered if he'd taken anyone. He felt for some reason for all his talk about women that he hadn't. When the bus stopped in front of Mr. Alex's house, Jack stood to get off and waited for his grandpa Tom. He sat.

"What is it, Grandpa Tom? What are you talking about?"

"Never mind. Jacky-boy, I love you. Now get off this here contraption so I can get me to work. And behave. Alex has a good heart we don't want to trample it with a bunch of questions, do we?" Jack shook his head.

With a quick kiss to his soft cheek, he got off the bus and walked up the driveway to the house. He hurried now. Jack couldn't wait to see his mom and tell her about his job. He walked into the kitchen, a place where he'd been meeting her since he'd been going to school.

After what seemed to him to be a hundred million hugs, she finally let him go. He was sitting in the chair in the kitchen. Jack watched his mom cut up the vegetables. Her hands were shaking and her face looked like she'd been bawling. He hated it when she cried because it made him feel so useless. He pulled out his papers and showed them to her.

"I got an A on my history exam today. The other kids were mad at me because I messed up the curve again. I didn't let it bother me." She read every answer on the test as he knew she would. "Do you think Mr. Alex will let me hang it on his refrigerator like we did at home?"

"I'm not sure, honey. This is a bachelor's home, not ours. He may not care for things on his refrigerator. Why don't we hang it someplace where he doesn't have to see it if he doesn't want to?" Jack took the paper back and put it with the others. What was the point of having a refrigerator if you couldn't hang papers on it?

"When you think we'll be leaving?" He saw her get hard in the back. He wished he hadn't asked. "I mean we can stay as long as Mr. Alex wants us too, right?"

"I don't know. I'm going to go find a job tomorrow. And Miss Caroline said I could come and work for her again. I'm going to be cleaning Mr. James' house too. That'll be our room and board. And we aren't guests here; we're only here because he's a generous man so you mind your manners."

Jack nodded. He looked down at the plate of veggies his mom always made sure he had when he came home from school. He didn't care for carrots, cooked or raw, but he ate them because she didn't want him to get sick. He played with one stick as he thought about his job.

"The guys who work here, Mr. Stone and Mr. Conley, they gave me a job the other day. They told me that I could work for them every weekend so long as you said it was okay." He continued when she didn't say no. "They said to tell you that I'd be safe with them. They are gonna show me how to make a living like a real man."

He heard her burst of laughter and it made him smile. "You won't be a pest to them, will you? They have a job to do too, you know?"

He was already nodding before she asked. "No, ma'am. Mr. Stone said I'd be fetching and towing for them. He said he'd buy me a root beer someday too. They paid me last week. Ten whole dollars."

"I think you mean fetching and toting for them. See that you mind your manners. And the money." Jack held his breath. He was sure she was going to tell him he had to save it all. "You make sure that you thank them for it."

# Chapter 14

Saturday dawned bright and cold. Heather had been in the house for three days and three nights now and was no closer to finding a job than she had been before. She was released to go back to the bakery on Monday morning and was very happy for it. The house was spotless from top to bottom because with nothing better to do, she'd been cleaning up. And she was still sleeping in the servant's room.

She tried to not think about his leaving her the other day. He'd not spoken of it since then and neither had she. In fact, they seldom spoke at all. She had been humiliated. More than that, she'd been hurt.

Now she was in the kitchen making muffins for the workers. She'd been up since before five and had already made several dozen. When she was upset, she had always turned to baking and she had been extremely upset. She turned to find Jack watching the back door for the first sign of his new boss.

"Mom, do you suppose I can be a construction worker when I grow up?"

She hid her smile.

"I mean, Mr. Stone owns his own company and everything. I think it would be cool."

"I'm sure you can do anything you set your mind to. But maybe you should wait until you're older and get a job on one of the crews. You might decide it's not for you. That's why teenagers get jobs in the summer. It's kind of like they're trying on jobs for later." She'd heard that on the news the other morning. "Besides, I think Mr. Stone might not like the competition."

Jack nodded. He was watching the door like it was going to burst open at any second. She wasn't sure what the men looked like that he'd worked for last weekend, but there were certainly enough of them around. He sat back down on the chair with a huff every time it opened and it wasn't the men. She could almost feel sorry for Mr. Stone. Jack had a list of questions to ask the man when he got here.

Heather looked up when Mr. James walked in. She didn't move when he started for her and when he reached around her for the coffee pot, she felt all the air in her lungs swish out. When he stood leaning against the counter drinking his coffee, she started to leave the room. He stopped her.

"Heather, if you don't mind, I'd like a word with you if you have a moment. I wanted to talk to you about the other day." She felt her face flame. "Could you meet me in the office?"

She nodded and walked down the hall just in front of him. She knew he was going to tell her that they had to leave because she wasn't keeping up her end of the bargain. When he closed the door behind him and she heard the lock click, she turned to face him.

"If you'd just give me to the end of next week, I'm sure I can find us a place to live. Grandda has been looking into the government subsi—"

"Please have a seat." She sat while he walked to the front of his desk and leaned against it. "I wanted to tell you how sorry I am about what happened Wednesday."

She looked up at him sharply. She'd expected him to be pissed, not apologize. When he smiled at her, she leaned back in the chair and looked up at him. "I don't understand." Her head was trying to make sense of what he'd just said.

"I'm telling you I'm sorry. I should never have tried…you'd just gotten home from the hospital and I was pawing at you like an animal. I'm sorry for that." He started pacing the room. "What I did was appalling. And I hope you can forgive me for it."

She waited for him to continue. To do something that would make her see what he was about. No one apologized for something that was offered freely, especially not to someone like her.

"So you don't want to have sex with me." He turned quickly at her statement. "Okay, but I need to find a way to pay for our staying—"

"I want you. I want you so badly that I can't sleep knowing that you're just down the hall from me. I can't think for wondering what you're doing, what you're wearing. Oh I want you all right. I don't want to, but I do." He sounded so pissed she felt her heart ache. "The problem is, what the hell am I supposed to do about it?"

Heather didn't answer. She wasn't sure what she could say to that anyway so she just let him rant. And rant he did.

"I've spent my whole life with knowing that I could have any woman I wanted, where I wanted, and how I wanted. I never had to question why, I just did. Then you come along." He started pacing again. "I don't know what the hell I'm supposed to do with you. Fuck you surely, but then what?"

"I didn't ask you to do anything with me. I made you an offer and you didn't have to accept it. If you want out of the bargain, then say so. I can go back to the shelter anytime I want." She stood up and moved to the door. "In fact, that's a perfect idea. Goodbye."

She got the door opened, but it slammed shut before she had a chance to go out it. His body was pressed hard against her and she could feel every part of him. When he rocked his cock into her ass, she moaned. Then she tried to pull away. He wasn't doing that to her again.

"Don't. Christ, don't." He rocked again, brought his hands around her waist, and cupped her breasts from behind. "Maybe if I can fuck you now, I can quit obsessing about you."

His breath was hot against her neck. She wanted to pull away. His words hurt deeper than anything before, but he bit her then laved the wound with his tongue. When he lifted her shirt off her and tossed to the floor, she felt her pussy clench. Need raced along her body as fast as his tongue did over her skin.

"Turn around. I need to taste you. Please, Heather, let me taste you." She turned for him and as soon as her back was pressed against the door, he had her nipple in his mouth and was sucking it hard.

Heather wound her fingers in his hair. She wasn't sure if she had been going to pull him away or to press him tighter against her. But when he slid his hand down the front of her pants, she nearly cried out.

"You're wet. And hot. I have to have you." Before she could say anything, do any more than take her next breath, he was on his knees before her and pulling her pants off.

She wanted to stop him, to try and slow him down. They were in the office, not in the bedroom. When he yanked off her panties, she tried to press her legs together and turn, but he held her still with his hands at her hips. Before she could make another attempt to get away, he took her into his mouth. It was all she could do not to scream.

"Please. You can't do that. It's not—" Her breath left her body in a hard moan.

~~~

It was too late now. He knew the moment that he'd touched her it was too late. He had to have her and be damned what happened later.

She tasted of honey, sweet and spicy, warm and delicious. He lapped at her, taking in her cream almost as quickly as it flowed from her. Sliding his hand up her thigh, he showed her that he wanted her legs apart, needed to touch her while he drank from her.

She was tight. Even as wet as she was, he felt how small she was and he knew in that moment that she'd not been with a man for a long while. Sliding his fingers deep, he opened her with them, stretching her for him because he was going to have her. When Alex felt her legs begin to tremble and buckle, he guided her to the floor and continued to feast while he pulled his pants open and freed his cock. Sitting up, he marveled again at her perfection as he opened the condom with his teeth.

Her eyes were glazed, her lips swollen from her teeth as she bit them. Sliding the condom over his cock, he leaned up and took her hardened nipple into his mouth and suckled. Her moan ran along his skin like she'd caressed him.

"Baby, I'm going to try and go slow, but you're so tight I don't know if I can. I'm sorry if I hurt you, but I need to be inside of you." She nodded, her hands reaching for him even as his cock sat at the mouth of her pussy. "Christ, I'm sorry."

He plunged forward. Her pussy wasn't just tight; it was a vise around him. He couldn't move she was strangling him so tight. He sat up to look down at her and wiped the tear from her cheek. She looked up at him then.

"You...you're inside of me." Her voice was low and husky. He rocked gently and watched her eyes flutter closed for just a second. "Please, I don't...you feel..."

She moved then. A small lift of her hips had him rocking deep again. When she did it again, he tried to hold her with his hips, but she wouldn't stop. Not wanting to hurt her anymore, he leaned down to whisper in her ear and ended up nipping her neck as she wrapped her legs around him.

Alex couldn't stop then. He moved deep again only to pull back and do it over again. Her sheath gripped him, and when he felt her climax begin, he knew that the moment she tumbled she was taking him with her. With her next rock up, he came, without much more warning than that he was throwing back his head and spilling himself deep within her. When the last of his tremors were finished, he dropped on her and tried to get his breathing and heart back to normal. It was several more minutes before he could move and then only to roll to his side.

Neither of them spoke. She laid there beside him and he could hear as her breath began to slow, but she said nothing. When she sat up and reached for her pants, he saw the tattoo on her lower back.

It was a rose, a deep red that was at the center of her spine. The blue ribbon he could see now was about two inches below her hips and seemed to say something. He rolled back toward her and read it. Colleen Heather Laird and two dates.

"Who is she?" She looked over her shoulder at him when he'd asked. "Colleen, Heather, who is she?"

She stood before answering. "My grandmother."

He waited for more, but she only continued to get dressed. He didn't know why he thought she should be willing to share this with him, but it pissed him off when she didn't.

"Heather, I was..." He realized she was pissed as well and picked up his own shirt. "This was your idea. You're the one that offered your body as payment." He knew it hurt her as soon as she turned toward him. He started to reach for her to apologize once again when she jerked back.

"Don't." She took a step back. "You're right of course. I'm sorry. If you'll excuse me—"

"Heather, I didn't mean to—"

"Mr. James, I would very much appreciate it if you'd just let me pass. I have to check on my son and there are things in the oven that I must attend to."

It was the "Mr. James," he decided. Had she called him Alex or even Alexander, he might have been all right. He grabbed her so quickly and had her pressed against the door again that he even surprised himself. But he was pissed now, beyond anything he'd been this far.

"You just had my cock inside of you. Calling me Mr. James is no longer an option. And I'll decide when we're finished, not you." He gave her a shake. "Tonight you'll be in my bed where I told you and every night until this is over, understand?"

She looked up at him, her eyes dark now with anger. She jerked her arm away from his and turned her back to him. He heard the small sob, but before he could react or say something to her, she had the door opened and was out.

Alex staggered to the chair and sat down hard. Putting his head in his hands, he looked down at the floor and at the empty condom wrapper. He'd taken her on the floor, taken her without regard to where they were because he'd wanted her. He looked up and closed his eyes. He wasn't even sure she'd enjoyed it.

Alex was still sitting in the chair when his cell phone rang. He groaned when he recognized the tone; it was his sister. He thought about letting it go to voicemail, but knew that if he did she'd just come over or better yet, call her husband and have him come and find him. He answered it on the fourth ring.

"Hey, I was wondering if I could borrow Heather for a few hours. I need to clean out my closet and I was going to see if she wanted any of the stuff."

"I'm not her keeper. You want to ask her shit like that then you call her, not me." He closed his eyes when she hissed at her end. "I'm sorry. I'm having a...Listen, call her on the house phone. I don't know where she's at, but somebody is bound to know where she's gone."

"Okay. But I deserve to know what the fuck that was about. Did you and her have a fight?"

He scrubbed his hand over his face. He knew his sister well enough to know that she was like a dog with a bone once she got something in her teeth. He could hang up on her and she'd come over and badger him or he could try to change the subject. Since that had never worked before, he was sure it wouldn't now. He thought his best plan was to simply tell her it was none of her business, but that too had never worked before so he just sighed and gave in.

"We had a fight. More like I had a fight and she took it. I was a prick and I took my shitty mood out on her." *After I fucked her on the floor*, but he didn't add that part.

"So you were your usual charming self and now she's…fuck, Alex, you had sex with her, didn't you?"

"How the hell did you figure that out from — damn it, Wills, that is none of your business. Damn it all to hell and back. Why can't you just leave things alone? I fucked up, all right. Is that what you want to here? She was there and I wanted her, so I took."

She was quiet for several seconds, long enough for him to realize what he'd said to his sister was true. He'd not cared a bit for what she'd wanted, only thought that he'd get her out of his system and make himself feel better.

"Is she all right?" Wills asked quietly. "Do you need me to come over and talk to her for you?"

"No. No, I screwed up. I'm the one who needs to fix this. I'm sorry I blew up on you." Her laugh made him smile.

"No worries, big brother. But the next time Jared and I have a fight, you have to take my side. Deal?" She laughed again. "Of course, that could more than likely be the end of the day, but hey, you never know."

He laughed again. "Thanks, sis. I love you." He closed his phone and went to find his jacket. It was time to see about his picture.

# Chapter 15

Mik listened to the idiot on the other end go on about what Alexander had been up to for the past twenty-four hours. The only thing that he'd failed to report on was the frequency of his bathroom breaks and the color and consistency of his stool when he had. Mik was about to hang up when he heard what he'd been looking for.

"The woman is there full-time now. Some broad. She comes and goes out of the house everyday at the same time. Seems she and the kid have a routine that is like clockwork."

"Who is she, do you know?" He picked up the pictures he'd had the fool take the other day and tried to figure out which woman it might be.

"Nah, don't know her name. She's real pretty. Tall and skinny, though. Long blondish-brown hair that she keeps pulled back in one of them braided ponytails. Her and the boy, I think they're related. She gives him a hug and a big ol' kiss everyday at the bus stop."

Mik picked up the picture of a woman out of focus and the boy from before. He couldn't tell shit from the pictures, but he would suppose she was pretty. He hoped she was something to Alexander. He was running out of time.

He had to get this job finished. He had no idea why he did, but it felt imperative that he get his money and get out of the country. Since the death of Wells, he'd been trying to figure out how to get the money moved from the accounts he'd tagged to his own account. So far all he'd managed to do was look at the other accounts and nothing more. He knew he could get them moved, but didn't have the know-how, just the resources to do it. That's were Alexander was going to help.

Brick had been helpful until he'd realized what was going on. Then he started to quote the contract at him and tell him that he'd not do anything illegal. When he threatened to go to the police, Mik had had to eliminate the problem. So now he was stuck.

But he was only stuck and not finished. The money had to be moved and moved soon. He wanted to be out of New York before winter hit hard and laying on a warm beach with white sand and blue water as soon as he possibly could. And Alexander James was going to make it happen for him. Whether he wanted to or not.

"Keep an eye on the woman and the kid. Don't make a move until I let you know. And you know what will happen to you if you're made, don't you?" Mik smiled when he heard the fool stutter.

"Yes, sir. I...me and my brother, we got it under control. Ain't a soul seen us. We've been being real careful like."

Mik set the phone in the cradle. He was going to be rich in just a matter of days. Looking around the room, he wondered what the person was thinking that had decorated this room. There wasn't really anything in here that reflected Mik's tastes, but he had wanted the house and with it came this room and several others he didn't care for.

He laughed when he remembered the face of the man who had lived here up until several weeks ago. Mik had come to the door and asked the man to move out. Mik had been polite, even asked twice. When the old man wouldn't do as Mik had wanted, well...it wasn't Mik's fault that the guy had to die. Moving out would have certainly given him a longer life. No, now he was living in a concrete pylon on the construction site.

Mik felt he was owed the finer things in life. Certainly the best he could steal. He'd given up the better part of his childhood to the system and had nothing. He'd had to fight his way out of the projects and then climb the ladder to be the best in his neighborhood. He'd had to claw, kill, and do whatever it took to get to where he was today. Yes, he thought, he deserved the best.

Going into the bedroom, he opened his closet and looked at the rows of Alfani and his grey sharkskin Michael Kors suits he'd have to leave behind when he left. He'd have no use for them on a beach. He had shoes, Hugo Boss and Cole Haan, all custom made for him. His ties were his most prized possession. He had perhaps four hundred of them, all name brands and some of them he'd never taken out of the box. Some women collected shoes, Mik collected ties.

And with all his collection, he was still not happy. He pulled out the picture he'd taken from his office. Alexander had gotten away. He'd also made of fool of Mik by not trusting him from the beginning. Mik traced a finger along the man's chest. He would shoot him here as soon as he had the money. Then he would spit on his body. No one fucked with Mikhail Black.

~~~

Willow liked Heather immediately. She wasn't sure what it was about her, but she did. She hated to use a cliché, but she had a quiet strength that made Willow want to stand beside her in a fight and protect her at the same time. And Willow could only hope to raise a son like hers. Jack was sitting very quietly at the dining room table doing his homework and eating a snack of carrot sticks and celery with a glass of milk.

"Where do you go to school at, Jack?" He glanced at his mother before answering. Cautious. She could appreciate that.

At her nod, he answered. "Mason School for the Gifted. I won a scholarship when I was six."

Willow looked up at Heather. "That's a great school. Alex went there too. He was seven, though. And he was in the...let me see, fifth grade when he was ten. How old are you?"

The kid had a grin that would melt hearts and his eyes were going to get women to fall all over him. "I'm not ten yet. I'm in the ninth grade. I have a photographic memory so I'm not really smart. I'm just very good at memorizing things."

"Jack, we talked about that. Remember?" Heather took his hand in hers and waited. "Tell her."

"I'm smart because I work hard and I want to succeed. I do too. I'm going to buy my mom a house she never has to fix things in and a car." He picked up his pen again. "And I'm not really smart, I just pretend to be." Heather burst out laughing. Willow did as well. The cheeky kid winked at her.

When the timer went off, Heather stood up and went to the kitchen. When she returned, she had a plate of chocolate chip cookies and another glass of milk. Willow could feel her mouth water and reached up to make sure there was no drool on her chin.

"That smell has been driving me crazy since I got here. I hope you're going to share." Willow reached for a hot cookie and tossed it back and forth in her hand to cool it off. "My dad said you were the best cook he's ever tasted."

"My mom doesn't eat cookies. She hates them." Jack picked up a cookie and without making a chocolate mess like she was, bit off a small bite and put it back down. "She doesn't like sweets at all."

"Jack, I'm sure Mrs. Stone doesn't give a fig about my eating habits. If you're done, please put your things away and do your chores. I'll be in soon."

They both watched as he left the room with another cookie. He kissed his mom on the cheek and told Willow it had been a pleasure meeting her. After he left, Willow looked over at Heather.

"He's a great kid. You've done well with him. And he's very handsome." Heather stood and began pacing. "What is it?"

"I don't know why you're here. I mean, I know it's your brother's house and all, but I told you he wasn't here. You said you wanted to give me clothes when any fool can see that I'd have nowhere to wear them. So I've been thinking that you came here for other reasons."

"I did. I wanted to meet you. I do have clothes for you. I'm going to have a baby in a few months and I wanted to clear some room out of my closet." Willow picked up another cookie and played with it. "And why do you think you'd have nowhere to wear them? Aren't you and Alex seeing each other?"

Heather stopped suddenly and sat down at the other end of the table about as far as one could get from Willow. "So that's it. I see. He's told you then. Well, I suppose that's okay, it's no secret. I would prefer you not tell Jack. He's too young to understand."

"Told me what?" Willow could feel the woman's anger. It was a palatable thing. "That you're living here? I'm pretty sure Jack knows that. I'm sure —"

"Told you that I'm his whore is what I mean. Yes, I can see that he did. When you have your baby, you'll see that a mother will do whatever it takes to keep a child safe." Heather looked at her hands on the table and Willow wasn't sure if she should be pissed or feel sorry for her. "I made my bed so to speak and I don't have a problem lying in it."

Willow didn't believe her. "I think you do. Has Alex done anything to make you...no, I'm not going to ask you that. I know my brother well enough to know that he wouldn't. What happened?"

Heather was quiet for so long that Willow wasn't sure she was going to answer. She continued to look out the window as she spoke, her voice soft and full of emotion.

"I was fourteen when my mother remarried. I never knew my father. He was...I'm not sure what he was, but if he spent more than an hour with my mother he had more than likely known enough to hide. Steven Baxter was his name — my step father I mean. From the very start he made me feel...I guess, dirty. He would open doors that I'd shut and walk in. He'd touch me...not in an adult to kid way, but personal."

"Did your mother know?" Willow asked her just as quietly. At Heather's nod, Willow decided to find the bitch and teach her a lesson in child rearing.

"I told her before they married and after. She never believed me. Or she did and didn't want to. I'm not...it doesn't matter. He kept at it and at it until I saved my money up and bought myself a lock to put on my door. But the more I developed, the more advanced his touches got. Until I turned fifteen. My birthday."

Willow didn't want to hear the rest. She was sure she knew what he'd done anyway. But she let the woman talk, afraid if she didn't then something vital would be lost between them.

"My mom had a charity thing to go to. I didn't go because I'd been grounded. Steven had grounded me on my birthday because of some injustice he'd said I'd done to him. He would tell my mom all sorts of things I'd done to be able to whip me. She put a stop to that after the second time he'd done it. But it didn't stop him from trying. He told me to eat my dinner then get to my room. I was happy to go. With the lock, I felt safe."

Willow got up and walked to the other end of the table and sat down across from her. Heather never looked up, nor did she seem to notice when Willow took her hands into her and held them. They were ice cold and clammy. The tears were there too and Willow doubted that Heather was even aware of them.

"I ate my dinner and put my dish in the sink. The glass I took with me to my room. I hated milk, but he told me to finish it. I started to feel sick almost right away. I just managed to get my door locked when I ran to the bathroom and started throwing up. After I'd sicked up all my dinner, I lay down on my bed and closed my eyes. It was the last thing I remembered."

"He got in, didn't he? He got into your room and raped you. The fucking bastard. Tell me where I can find him and I'm going to castrate him for you. Hell, for all women. And your mother too. She needs someone to teach her a lesson or two." Willow hadn't meant to speak out loud, but just thinking about the little girl Heather had been made her mad enough to murder.

"Yes, he got in. When I woke up...when I woke up, I was tied to the bed. He'd taken all my...I was naked. I don't know how long I was out. I guess it had been a while. He'd busted down my door, you see. It lay against the doorway broken. The gag in my mouth prevented me from screaming, but I did try. I swear to you that I did."

Willow wasn't surprised at the venom in her voice. What she was surprised about was her need to say it. Willow would bet her last dollar that Heather's mother had accused her of that and had told everyone that she'd let the man do it.

"I know you did. I know it. Go on, honey, tell me the rest." Willow held her hands while Heather continued.

"He told me...he told me that he'd done it before. That he only married women with virgin daughters. He said that he didn't really care for my mother, but she was a means to an end. A way to...I was just the prize, he'd said." Heather wiped at the tears before she continued. "He raped me, but he didn't hurt me. I mean, he could have. I had no way of...there wasn't any way for me to fight him. But he didn't...do you understand?" Willow nodded. "My mother didn't. She told me that she wished he'd killed me."

"Christ. She's a real peach, your mom." Heather didn't say anything as she continued.

"After the trial, I was—"

"He went to jail? Hot damn, there is justice after all. How long does he have? I'm hoping he has at least five more lifetimes left."

Heather smiled before answering. "He's dead. He was killed in prison not long after Jack turned one. I read about it in the paper. My mother blamed me for that as well." Willow let go of Heather's hands when she pulled away. "I found out about Jack a few weeks later. I didn't tell anyone. I suppose I should have, but I knew that she'd...my mother would make me get rid of him. She didn't want anything to remind her of what I'd put her through. As it was, she'd changed her name back to her maiden name as she'd done after my father left. Or so she said. I'm not sure if she was married to him, but that's neither here nor there. But the shame of me being pregnant was too much, I guess. And she threw me out."

Willow was sure there was much more to it than that—a child of fifteen pregnant and alone, a mother screaming at her to get rid of him. Willow's assessment of the woman went up several notches. Willow wasn't sure she would have been able to do it at that age, even as smart as she was.

"I'm not sure why I told...you must think I'm a very whiny person, don't you? I don't blame you. I've never told that to anyone before. Not all of it anyway. The police, I guess, and Jack knows some of it. But I've never told anyone before. I'm sorry. I do hope you can forgive me." Heather stood and Willow with her. "I should go and check on Jack. He's got school tomorrow."

Willow pulled her into her arms and hugged her. Heather was stiff at first, but after a few seconds, she leaned into her and hugged her back. "I don't think you're whiny. I think you're one of the bravest people I know."

Willow left an hour later. Their friendship was new to them both and tender, but they both seemed easier around each other. Heather took the clothes, though she told her that she wouldn't wear most of them. She'd told Willow that she wasn't a fancy person. The pile of clothes mostly consisted of jeans and flannel shirts.

# Chapter 16

Alex looked at the letter again as it lay on his desk. Brick had known that he was going to be killed. Known and had said nothing to him. He'd even been afraid that Amy would be as well. He picked it up and read it again.

*Dear A,*

*If you're reading this, you are either an incredibly nosey bastard or I'm dead. I'm hoping it's the first, but I'm reasonably sure it's not.*

*First, I wanted to tell you that I'm sorry. I should have listened. Mik is into some major shit and he only wanted us, or me I guess, because he figured as a young company, we'd be better to take the fall than he would. He's taking robbing banks to a whole new level.*

*Attached you'll find a list of all the accounts that he plans to hit. I'm not as slick as you are, but I can work my way through a computer given enough time. He doesn't know I have it. At least I hope not. He has this idea that the money can be moved from the accounts without anyone being the wiser and we (yes, he said he would take Amy and me with him) would be long gone before anyone was the wiser. Fat chance, right?*

*I know you're a smart guy. You got the brains and as I'm sure you know, I got the looks. Help me make my death worth something. And I'm begging you to please watch out for him.*

*Amy will need you. I'm asking you as my best friend to make sure she's okay. I love her so very much and wish that I could have more time with her. If you ever get the chance to find that special someone in your life, grab on with gusto. You never know when everything will be taken from you in a heartbeat.*

*I love you, buddy, not in the "I wanna sleep with you" kind of way, but you are my best bud. Live long and prosper.*

*B.*

Alex looked at the accounts. There were ten of them and as of nine days ago, the total amount in the accounts was just under one hundred million dollars. Along with the account numbers and names was another number. Brick thought it was a Swiss bank account routing number.

Mik was going to come for him, Alex was sure of this. He'd had no doubt whatsoever. He would have to figure that either Brick had talked to him or that he would have left him something. Alex felt he'd watched enough shows on television to know this much. Now he had to figure out what to do and who to get help from.

His dad had friends everywhere so that would be his first guess in getting help. Alex reached for his phone only to stop before touching it. Bugs. Pulling out his cell phone, he started to call him that way when he thought again about someone recording him, so he opened his phone and texted him.

Within minutes he and his dad arranged to go Christmas shopping at the mall in the morning. Alex didn't even ask for his dad not to tell his mom. His parents had always told each other everything and he didn't doubt this would be any different. When the knock came to his door, Alex nearly snapped for whoever it was to go away. But he yelled for whoever it was to come in.

"Hi, Mr. Alex. I was wondering if I could ask you a question, please?" Jack didn't move away from the doorway. "I promise I won't take up much of your time."

Alex waved him in then watched as Jack turned and closed the door. *Must be serious*, Alex thought, and wondered if this was something he should refer to his mom. As Jack settled in one of the chairs across from him, Alex wondered how to broach the subject when Jack spoke.

"I've been working for Mr. Conley and Mr. Stone on Saturdays. My mom gave me permission," he hurriedly said. "They said it was pocket money. I had to look that up at school."

Alex leaned back in the chair, thinking this he could handle. "They're good men, some of the best I've ever known. Are you hoping for a raise already, Jack?"

Alex watched the boy's face change from pleasure to fear in an instant. "No, sir. I swear. I just wanted to buy my mom something for Christmas."

Wondering if he would ever feel more like shit than he did right now, Alex sat up in the chair. First, he manhandles the boy's mother then treats her like a cheap date. Then let's not forget that he treats a kid he genuinely likes as if he…Alex took a deep breath. "I'm sorry, Jack. I was only teasing you. Let's start again, shall we? What did you have in mind to get her?"

Jack didn't say anything for several minutes, but continued to look down at his hands. Alex got up and went around the desk. When he was seated in the other chair, Jack turned to look at him.

"We lost everything in the fire. But Mom said we should be grateful we got out." Alex nodded. "But she worked so hard on it and now it's all burned up. It's not fair, don't you think, Mr. Alex?"

"Anything you work really hard for and lose because of something you had no control over is hard. What is it she lost?" Alex thought if it was something small or even something Jack had given her, Alex decided that he'd get it for him and see that she got it. Then he realized that Jack had said that she had *earned* it.

"Her diploma. She had it on the fridge. We would hang our papers there when we'd do well. I hung it there for her when she wouldn't. But she didn't take it down."

"Her diploma?" Alex remembered his mom hanging art and good grades on theirs as well. He wondered what sort of diploma Heather had gotten.

"Yes, sir. She couldn't finish high school because of me see so she went to one of those courses by mail. We made sure it was accredited and all. Mom wants to go to college. She said she didn't want me to be ashamed of her. Not that I would, she's wonderful and very smart."

"Yes, she is," Alex answered absently. High school diploma. "What is it you hand in mind then?"

Jack stood up, dug out a neatly folded sheet of paper from his pocket, and handed it to him. "I have the name of the school and the dates it had on it. I wanted to see if they can print another one for her. Then I want to get it framed. She told me that she wanted to do that when we got a house of our own."

Alex looked at the paper. From the dates, it looked like she must have been at it a long while. He looked up at Jack when he started talking again.

"She worked really hard. Sometimes I'd help her with her math homework, but she would keep at it until she understood it. It was hard with her working three jobs all the time. But she refused for us to be on welfare. She told me if a person is able-minded and body sound that there is no reason for them to be taking a handout when so many others could use it."

Alex nodded. This wasn't the picture he had painted of her. Her mother made her sound selfish and cold. She told him she was a horrible mother and even went so far as to hint that she may sell herself or her child for drugs. Alex could see from looking at him that Jack was a well-adjusted and healthy kid. And he didn't think he'd ever seen or heard a more polite young man.

"Your grandmother, do you ever see her?" Alex tried to remember her name. "Shelly, I think her name is."

"Vickie. And no, she hates me. A lot," Jack said with a bite in his voice.

"I doubt that she hates you. She might be upset about—"

"She told my mom if she got rid of me then she would help with our bills and stuff. She made my mom cry when she said it. Grandpa Tom said she wasn't any daughter of his anymore. That made Mom cry harder." Jack brushed at a tear. "Grandpa Tom told me they didn't raise her to be like that, Vickie, I mean. He said he and Grandma Colleen are good people and she should be glad her mom wasn't alive or Grandma Colleen would bust her bottom but good."

~~~

Heather was just empting the dishwasher when she heard someone come into the room. Thinking it was Jack, she had a smile already in place. It faded to a frown when she saw Mr. James.

"Well that's very telling."

She frowned harder, not understanding him.

"I'd like to speak to you, please. Privately."

"Grandda has already gone to bed and Jack in is the room you assigned him. He knows to go to bed at nine-thirty. So you can say what you want. Oh." She walked to her bag on the floor and picked it up, taking out an envelope. "The Red Cross gave this to me today. They said it was for room and board and to get us back on our feet. It's five hundred dollars."

She handed it toward him only to have him back up. She didn't have the energy to fight with him so she laid it on the table. She picked up a dish cloth and starting wiping down the already clean counter.

"I don't want your money, Heather. Keep it. Use it to get some of your Christmas done." She glanced up to see if he was serious. "I won't take money from you."

She didn't say anything, but she hurt. He'd rather humiliate her with sex than take her money. Well, she'd already decided that's all he'd get was just sex. She was going into this with her eyes wide open. She just hoped her heart would stay closed.

"I've made myself a budget. I'm thinking we should be out just after mid-January. It might have been sooner, but the landlord said I'm not entitled to my deposit back. It wasn't much, but it would have helped us. Grandda is trying to pick up more hours what with the—"

"Sit down please."

His clipped order made her stop speaking. She also stopped moving, not realizing that she'd been pacing. She sat in the chair at the table and put her hands in her lap so that he wouldn't see them tremble. "There's no need for you to talk to me like that. I'm sorry you don't want us here, but I did offer for us to return to the shelter."

She heard him swear and nearly smiled. He could string them together as well as her grandda could. When he went to the refrigerator, she looked up then back down when she saw him bent over peering inside. The man was something to look at when he did that. She felt her face heat up and her body tighten thinking about him being deep inside of her. How he'd tasted her. She shifted on the chair, suddenly uncomfortable.

"Is this tea sweet?"

It took her mind several seconds to realize he'd asked her a question about something. But for the life of her she couldn't make her mind work out what he'd said for the lust running through her body. "I'm sorry," she said, licking her suddenly dry lips. "What did you say?" He stared at her as she was staring at him and with another oath, he slammed the fridge door closed and yanked her to him. His mouth was on hers before she could take a breath. Then she didn't want to.

Like before when he'd kissed her, she marveled at his taste. Warmth and hunger, need and tenderness exploded in her mouth. When his hands cupped her and brought her flush with him and his erection, she felt her pussy swell, need coil, and a hunger of her own spiral out of control.

His mouth pulled from hers and she whimpered. But he was no less busy with it. He nipped at her neck and her shoulder; his tongue slid over her pulse that she could feel hammering at her throat. When he picked her up, she felt weightless and needed. With his mouth over hers again, she didn't even realize that they'd climbed the stairs and entered his room. The mattress at her back was a startling realization.

He stripped off his shirt then his shoes. She watched, memorized, as he unbuckled his belt, and her mouth watered for what he was going to reveal to her, for her. His groan had her looking up at his face. She flushed as his knowing grin.

"Unless you want me to rip those clothes to shreds, I would suggest that you take them off." She didn't move, her body seemingly frozen at his words. "Now, Heather."

She stood, pulled her t-shirt over her head, and dropped it on the floor. She didn't have any shoes on so she unbuttoned her pants and shimmied them off with her socks all at once. She stood before him in her bra and panties, suddenly unsure.

He was naked, beautifully so. His cock was hard and straining from his dark curls at his groin. She wanted to touch him, see if he was as hard as he looked. Without thinking about what he'd do to her, she reached out and wrapped her hand around him.

Smooth, was her first thought, then hard. Incredibly so. When she ventured her hand up and down him, she jerked her hand back when he hissed at her.

"I'm so sorry. I...I didn't—"

"Don't stop. Touch me, Heather." He took her hand and rubbed her knuckles up and down his cock then turned her hand over to show her how to touch him. "Your hand is so cool against me. So different than when I'm inside of you where you're hot and so wet."

She stepped closer to him and felt his heat. When he unclasped her bra and peeled if from her shoulders, his mouth followed the straps down. When her panties joined her bra and other clothes, he stepped back and stared at her so much so that she reached up to cover herself. But he stopped her.

"No. Don't. Let me look. The last time was so quick that I...Christ, you're beautiful."

She felt that way too. When he told her to lie down, she did without any hesitation. When he stretched out beside her, she felt her body respond—her nipples tightened and her pussy seeped so much so that she pressed her thighs together.

He stopped her with his hand. "I want to feel you wrapped around me. Feel your tight pussy when you come. Would you like that, love, to feel my cock buried deep inside of you?"

"Yes. Oh yes, please." He took her nipple into his mouth as he moved between her legs. She cried out when he bit her. Her body surged up to take him into her, but he was too far away. "Please," she begged again.

"Condom," he growled. "Christ, I want...I have to hurry now." The condom slipped from his fingers twice and when he finally got it open, he had to roll it over the tip twice as he was so wet. Heather ran her thumb over his tip and took the pearl of cum into her mouth. Alex froze above her.

His eyes were black, sweat beaded above his lip and brow like he was working very hard. The pulse at his throat was pounding. She wasn't sure she'd ever seen a more beautiful sight than him at that moment. She gasped when he slammed into her. Her legs wrapped around him and she surged up with his next move. The pressure, the building, was close, so close she could almost touch it. When her climax took her, took her to heights she'd never seen, never dreamt of, she screamed out his name. Clawing at his back, she felt him stiffen then felt him come. His body pounded into hers even as she felt hers slide into a state of satiation.

# Chapter 17

Alex woke alone in his bed. Pulling the clock next to his bed closer to him, he was surprised to see it was nearly nine o'clock. He hadn't slept that late in years. Getting up, he headed for the shower.

His clothes were folded nearly in the chair by the fireplace, he noticed. Even his shoes were straightened up. Alex smiled when he thought of Heather's son being just as compulsively neat. He was using the toilet when he realized something else.

The condom was broken.

Grabbing the counter for support, he closed his eyes against the implication of his find. He'd been inside of her, came inside of her naked, bare and without protection.

"Mother fuck," he murmured. He wondered if she knew, if she had any idea when she'd left his bed. He doubted it, but still, it grated on his nerves and mind.

In his heart, he knew she didn't plan this. In his heart, he knew there wasn't any way for her to have been able to tear the condom, but his mind was fertile with deceit and betrayal. He tore off the broken latex and actually toyed with the idea of confronting her with it when his cell phone rang.

"You know, son, when we go shopping together it usually means we're in the same place at the same time when it happens. Usually, but I could be wrong."

"Shit, Dad, I forgot. I'm getting in the shower now. I'll be there in twenty minutes tops." He tossed the condom in the trash and turned on the shower.

He was jerking on fresh jeans when he saw the envelope on his dresser. She'd brought up something after she'd left his bed. He had no idea why that pissed him off more, but he was sort of glad there was no one in the kitchen when he got down there. But he did want to speak to her. After he made love to her again...provided he didn't strangle her first. He was nearly to the mall when his phone rang again. This time, it was Caroline.

"The new pans came this morning. Did you know there are different types of pans for different kinds of ovens?" She laughed. "Seems I have a lot to learn about my own shop."

"I suppose, like you, I thought they were all the same. You slap some dough on them and pop them in the oven. I take it they're not." He parked his car next to his dad's and rubbed his suddenly aching head.

"Hummm, apparently not. Heather said that we need—"

"Heather? Heather is there? Now? Why?" He took a deep breath when he heard the tone of his own voice. "Do you think I could speak to her, please?"

There was a shuffle of movement, a voice muffled. He waited for what seemed an eternity then he heard her breathing. His heart picked up the pace as he thought about her.

"Hello," she answered.

Alex felt his cock harden at the sound. He was wondering what the hell was wrong with him when he spoke again. "I didn't know you'd been released to return to work. When did that happen and why wasn't I informed?" Closing his eyes, he tried to regain control of his temper before he pissed her off. Too late, he realized when she snapped back at him.

"Listen here, you arrogant, one-celled microscopic organism. I do not answer to you. I don't answer to anyone as a matter of fact. I sleep with you. I fuck you. Period. And as soon as I can arrange it, I'm not even going to do that. Of all the…I'm hanging up now before I say something…Oh you make me so mad." Then the phone went dead.

Alex had to set the phone down gently or risk shattering it and his window. When he felt he had a semi better hold on his anger, he picked up his phone and got out of his car. His dad was waiting in the food court.

"So…do you want to talk about it or stew on it some more first?" Alex looked at his dad, confused. "We've been shopping for the past hour and all you've done is check your phone and mutter about women and sex. Which I might point out to you I wouldn't repeat any of in front of your sister or your mother. Either one of them will take exception to it."

Alex looked at his watch. Christ, he'd been here an hour and ten minutes. The woman was driving his insane. He started to say something to his dad and decided not to.

"I don't want to talk about it. I need someone to help me with a few accounts—do you know she had the nerve to call me an amoeba?" Alex glared at his dad when he burst out laughing. "I was just asking if...I don't want to talk about her."

Alex picked up a mixer and wondered if Heather would like it. She loved to cook. The dinner she'd made for them all last night had been wonderful. Of course he wasn't sure he'd actually been supposed to be invited. Jack had insisted and he had joined them.

"What kind of accounts are we talking? Corporate or domestic? It'll make a difference on who I ask to help you out. I take it this is about Brick's murder."

Alex nodded at his dad and picked up a food processor. "Mostly corporate, but one domestic. All of them moneyed. There are—she went to work today. All I did was ask her if she was cleared. She seems to take exception to every little thing I say to her." He slammed the food processor down.

"Hummm and what did she say to your asking? I'm just thinking, just thinking mind you, that if you snarled at her like you just did then she might have pointed out you're sleeping with her and nothing more."

Alex answered before thinking. "That's just what she said. Then she hung up on me."

His dad's grin made him flush. Alex couldn't believe what he'd just admitted. He picked up the first item he touched to keep himself from looking at him. He was a grown man, almost thirty-one years old, and he had just embarrassed himself like he was ten again.

"She's a lovely girl and has had a tragically hard time since her mother threw her out."

Alex bobbled the box. "Threw her out? No. Mrs. Laird said...how did you hear she'd been thrown out?"

His dad picked up a platter and inspected it as if he was going to buy stock in the company. By the time he answered, Alex was ready to brain him with it.

"Oh she and Wills had a long talk night before last. She told Wills about the rape on her birthday and everything."

The box bobbled again, this time nearly hitting the floor. If not for his dad grabbing it up, it would have broken that and several others as well. Alex simply started at his dad.

"Rape?" He realized he'd been a little loud when several people looked his way. He lowered his voice. "Rape? No, no, no. She was…damn it, why didn't she tell me? I have a right to know she was raped. Was it Baxter? I'm going to kill the bastard."

His dad picked up the food processor Alex had sat down and was reading the front of the box. Alex was reasonably sure he'd go to prison for murder if his dad didn't stop shopping and talk to him.

"I'm going to buy this for Heather for Christmas. I believe she'll like it, don't you think? And yes, it was Baxter. But you don't have to worry about killing him, he's dead. Killed in prison when Jack was a year old."

Alex took the box from his dad. "No you won't be buying my Heather this. Tell me what she told Wills. And is Jack really his?"

His dad took the gift back. "Yes, Jack is his child. Thank God he had nothing more to do with the boy other than to sire him. He might not have been smart enough to attend your alma mater. Kid's a freshman at ten, do you believe it? I can't wait to meet him. Anyway, Wills said that Heather's mother kicked her out at fifteen. I can't imagine your mom or me doing such a horrific thing, can you? Poor girl."

Alex hadn't known, hadn't even tried to know. And instead of asking Heather her side of the story, he'd simply went with the one her mother had told him.

"I'm a fool. And a jackass. I don't deserve her."

Edgar shifted the box in his arms. "Do you want her, son?"

Did he? He'd never been so unsure of something in his entire life. Not even his first wife had he felt like this. But he did know one thing, he needed to talk to her and very soon.

They did some more shopping while they talked about the real reason for them being there. His dad was going to give someone he knew the information about the accounts and see what he could do about them. Alex said he was going to keep it close to the vest and not to talk to Mik if he could help it.

His dad got Heather the food processor and Alex bought her mixer and all the attachments that went with it. All he could think about on his way home was now where was she going to use it?

~~~

Mik took his plane to Ohio. He'd been hearing from the idiots almost daily and he wasn't happy with the way things were going. Alexander had visited the widow in the hospital twice, which might not have concerned him except for the fact that she had disappeared soon after. Idiot One had said he'd gone to the hospital to get rid of her when he'd been informed by the nurse on duty she'd been moved.

"And there ain't no budging her on more information either. She was scary." Mik wanted to point out that he carried a gun, which by all accounts should have made him scarier, but didn't. The headache forming behind his eyes was enough to deal with for the moment.

Alexander had also gone to the offices. That in and of itself should have been fine too, but he'd gone to a safe Mik didn't know anything about. That pissed him off more because Brick, who he was supposed to trust, hadn't told him about it. Mik wanted to dig him up and shoot him all over again. Mik had gone to a great deal of expense bugging and putting in cameras to have something like that go unnoticed.

He just knew the cock sucker wasn't to be trusted. Now he had to figure out what, if anything, Brick had left his former partner. He didn't like that he had been fooled. Nope, not one bit.

He had the driver take him to the best hotel then laughed out loud when he pulled up in front of the James Suites. Wouldn't do to have his prey find out he was in town before he was ready so he pulled out another ID and checked in. He'd forgotten it was Thanksgiving the day after tomorrow and was glad he'd made a few calls before coming here.

Mik hated that he couldn't find fault with the service thus far. And it pissed him off more that he couldn't find anything wrong with his room. But it was early yet so he'd bide his time. When the porter left without a tip, Mik got a charge out of the man's obvious disappointment.

Renting a car was easy enough. He'd had to lighten his cash a bit to get it, but he wasn't out anything. The hundreds were counterfeit and the card he'd used belonged to the man's house he was living in. Smiling for the first time in months, Mik drove to Alexander's house where the gates were left wide open for him.

Construction workers were everywhere. It seemed the place was overrun with them. Mik had told several of the men that he'd encountered that he was there to inspect permits. He'd been shown all the work they'd been doing and each permit to do the work. He enjoyed the ruse so much he nearly missed one of the workers comment on how Mr. James wouldn't be retuning until Sunday evening.

He drove back the hotel mad. The nerve of the bastard, Mik thought. Didn't he have better things to do at home? Mik couldn't find out where he'd gone no matter how much he'd tried. Stone Construction was very loyal to their clients — fucking assholes.

Prepared to wait him out, Mik found himself a nice place to have dinner and proceeded to make plans. As the night grew shorter, so did his temper and patience. By ten o'clock, Mik was ready to deal with Alexander on Mik's terms and damn the man for fucking things up for him.

# Chapter 18

Victoria Laird looked at the letter from her father again. He'd disowned her. And while that didn't bother her as much as it did him, the man was going to make it public and that just wouldn't do.

Victoria felt as if enough of her little issues had been made public, thank you very much, and she certainly didn't want this little tid-bit to be out there as well. She shuddered when she thought about how she'd been treated in the public eye recently. Why should anyone care how her workers were treated? They were paid, were they not? If people would just leave her alone and do things the way she wanted them done, there would be no more problems.

First there had been the little incident with her first husband. Well, she'd never actually been married to David Wilson, but anyone who could remember that had been dealt with. Of course her parents, now just her father, didn't know she hadn't been, but that was just fine too. But when she'd found out she'd been knocked up by him after she'd thrown him out...well, she certainly wasn't going to ask him to come back. Besides, he wasn't worthy husband material anyway.

Then there had been Heather Colleen. She'd been a beautiful child, so malleable and easy to control and mold into the perfect daughter. Then she'd had to ruin it all by saying Steven had raped her. Victoria looked at the letter on her desk blotter. And now this.

Victoria had seen the way Steven had looked and watched her daughter. She'd noticed that he'd touch her in ways that made her daughter cringe. Even after Heather Colleen had come to Victoria, she'd done nothing about it except not allow him to spank her any more. Victoria chose, like she did all things she didn't want to deal with, or didn't like, to ignore it. Then when Heather Colleen had bought the lock, Victoria thought the matter was solved. And it cost her nothing.

Victoria thought back to the day she'd come home to find Heather Colleen's door off the hinges. She'd been furious with her daughter thinking she'd locked herself out of her room and had had to break down the door to get in. But as she entered the hall outside the bedroom, Victoria had been shocked to silence by what she'd seen.

Heather Colleen had been tied to the bed. Her arms above were lashed to the headboard and her legs, wide open, had been secured to the legs of the bed. She was naked except for a gag in her mouth and even from the doorway, Victoria could see the tears.

Steven was just rising from the bed just as naked as her daughter. His spent cock was still covered in blood from what Victoria knew was her daughter's virginity. Neither of them, Steven nor Heather Colleen, noticed her.

"You were so tight, darling, tighter than I ever had before. Maybe I'll do this again before I let you go.

Maybe." Steven ran his hand up and down his hardening cock. "You're a much better pussy then your fat cow of a mother. But I had to marry her to get to you. What I really wanted anyway."

His cock was hard now and Victoria could hear her daughter's screams. Before Victoria could move, Steven continued talking. And what he said made her madder than what he'd done to her daughter.

"Of course I'm not really married to her. There are many, many more wives before her and I'm sure many after. I like virgins, you see, and take my prize from the hapless and often time ugly mothers before I move on to the next gift the girl has to offer me."

Heather Colleen looked right at her and started screaming. Steven turned quickly and backed away from the bed, grabbing up the first thing he could to cover himself.

"She lured me in here," he claimed hastily. "You can't blame a man for being weak when she throws herself at me day and night." Victoria didn't say anything but looked at her daughter. "She wanted me to tie her up. She said...she said it was a game she played. She did this, not me."

Victoria picked up the first heavy object she could reach and threw it. She hadn't been aiming at anything in particular and thought it was just blind luck that the glass paperweight hit him in the forehead. Steven dropped like dead weight.

Calling the police had been automatic, she thought now. She hadn't wanted his corpse on the floor and thought it was the best way to deal with it. She knew now, however, that if she had to do it all over, she wouldn't have. She would have just thrown him out and bundled

Heather Colleen up and taken her away. But by the time the ambulance had arrived and the first police cruiser, it was too late.

The lawyer told her it was a slam dunk case. His semen and her blood on him had been about all they'd needed to put him away. Of course the dozen or so girls, some in their late twenties by then, had come forward as soon as the news broke about him. They all claimed the same thing. He'd raped them by tying them to the bed and after taking their virginity, he'd beaten them, threatened them to silence, and left.

Heather Colleen had been kept out of it for the most part. She'd been a minor then so without Victoria's permission, they couldn't question her and by the time the trial was going, Victoria had already thrown her out. Her daughter wouldn't do what she wanted so she had meant to teach her a lesson. She didn't count on her having a backbone or worse yet, Victoria's father to stepping in to help her out. When she thought of him being there for the granddaughter and not his own daughter, Victoria would get angry all over again.

A runaway, she'd told everyone. The news and the media had driven Heather Colleen to run and Victoria could only hope her daughter wouldn't become one of the thousands of other runaways and show up dead. The sympathy that Victoria had gotten from that had been delicious and she had milked it for all she was worth.

Then when she'd had Steven killed while he'd been in prison, she'd gotten a lot more. A wealthy man like him gone wrong, the papers had said. Too bad Heather Colleen couldn't be here to hear the news, Victoria had told one reporter. That had lasted for another year or so.

Victoria's biggest fear was that someone would find her daughter or worse yet, she'd come forward with her brat. Victoria had tried for years to get Heather Colleen to get rid of it, but she would always refuse. And now this man...James somebody was asking questions.

She didn't think it was a coincidence that her father and this James person were to contact her at the same time. They were in this together, she just knew it. Something...anything to make her life more difficult, and she just wouldn't have it.

Heather Colleen was at her lies again. Her daughter was talking to this—Victoria looked down at the other letter she'd received and saw that his name was Alexander—person and stirring up trouble again. Well, Victoria was smarter and much more finically secure than her daughter; she'd made sure of that. It was time to take action, to make sure that this man wouldn't believe her daughter, but only her. Things she couldn't undo were depending on no one finding out that Victoria had tossed her unwed pregnant daughter out and had known all along where she'd been.

Victoria was wondering if she should find this man and show him what a horrible person her daughter was. Unless of course she could convince Heather Colleen to shed herself of the abomination, the child she'd had out of wedlock, and come back to live with her. She would forgive the child if she would only do what she said. Victoria wasn't concerned if she and her father mended fences or not. He'd be dead soon enough so what did it matter to her? Picking up the phone, she decided to take matters into her own hands and pay a little visit to Mr. James.

"Wallace," she said to the butler when he answered the phone. "Pack a bag for me. I'm going to Columbus for a few days."

"It's Henry, ma'am. And of course. Shall I make arrangements for you to stay somewhere then?"

She closed her eyes. Did he really expect her to remember his name? What the hell was she paying people for, so she could be their buddy?

"I believe that would ensure you keeping your job for a bit longer if you do." She hung up knowing that as soon as she returned, she'd be replacing Wallace, or Henry, or whatever the hell his name was.

~~~

Alex parked outside the bakery at near closing and looked inside. They were busy. The door was barely closed before someone else was opening it again. He hated to admit it, but he was nervous. He looked over at Tom.

"She ain't gonna hurt you with a store full of people. Best go in and face the music, son. Me and Jacky-boy will be waiting out here for you."

Alex wasn't encouraged by Tom's assurances that she wouldn't hurt him. He was pretty sure she would, and he didn't know if he didn't deserve it or not. He looked at the store front again and wondered if he should start out by telling her how sorry he was or to just simply go in on his hands and knees and beg.

Alex had picked up Tom at work and together, they'd gone to get Jack. Alex's mom had told him to bring them all to Thanksgiving dinner at her house. Apparently, his dad had told her everything. Everything they'd talked about at the mall.

"You'd do well to make this girl happy, Alexander. She sounds like someone I could like and you know how much you already do. Make this work, all right?"

Alex had gone straight to the library and read the newspaper clippings about the trial and how the minor had run away. Heather's name hadn't been mentioned, but Alex had known it was her. Then he'd gone to the courthouse and found someone his mom knew, and was able to purchase a transcript of the trial as well. Even skimming over it, he knew enough now to surmise that Baxter had raped her and he'd deserved to die.

Now he was ready to do whatever he needed to make it up to Heather. Because sometime between the time he'd met her and now, he'd fallen in love with her. He was pretty sure his mother had known it before him.

"Do you think she has any sharp knives or weapons in there with her? Not that I don't deserve her hurting me, but still. My mom will be really disappointed if I die during the holidays." He was half kidding and was really surprised when Jack giggled behind him.

Alex thought he couldn't love a kid more than he did this one and turned in his seat to talk to him. "Think maybe you should come in and be my bodyguard? It might soften her up a bit to see you first."

"Mom won't hurt you much. You have to watch out for her foot, though. She taps it when she's mad. The faster it goes, the madder she is at you. And her brows, watch them too."

When Jack didn't elaborate, Alex looked at Tom before asking. At his shrug, he turned back to Jack. "What about her brows, buddy. Do they flame up or something?"

"No, sir, they raise. Like her temper. Grandpa Tom said that it was like a barometer, the higher the pressure, the higher they go. If they go all the way to her hair, then you are gonna be grounded for a long time."

Jack had sounded so sincere that Alex couldn't laugh. It had been hard, but he managed to just keep it under control. He got out of the car and went inside, knowing that her brows were going to be at her hairline if not a little higher.

Alex saw Caroline first. She was grinning at him. "If you've come to piss her off more, I may have to kiss you."

That stopped him. "Why? And why do you think I—" He stopped talking when her brow rose.

Alex was going to ask his dad about that one. Were women's brows sort of an indicator for men to know just when to shut the fuck up? He was going to have to pay more attention to his sister too.

"You did and you very well know it. She said she bakes when she's stressed or mad. I would say from her muttering and her output that you've done something really bad." She looked him up and down. "And you without a single flower or a box of candy. You must be going back there as a dead man is all I can figure."

"Flowers. I should…where can I get her some?"

He was backing toward the door when he saw her. All thoughts of flowers and eyebrows fled his mind. Before he knew it, he was pulling her into his arms. What he should have remembered about her was the brows and the foot.

The head to the nose was completely unexpected, as was her foot coming down on the top of his. By the time he'd backed away, his shirt was covered in blood and he was sure his nose was broken. When she started toward him, he nearly fell over the chair behind him trying to get away.

"Sit down," Heather snapped. He sat. He was actually afraid not to. This was a side of her he'd not seen and he wasn't altogether sure he liked it. "What do you think you're about? You've no right to kiss me or to touch me here. I'm working."

He hissed when she put a wet towel on his face none too gently. Even with his face throbbing, he could see her brow up high and he could hear her foot tapping a mile a minute. He might have laughed, but he was a tad terrified she'd kill him.

"I didn't mean to touch you, but—"

"Then what were you thinking? Hum? Or were you? No, don't answer that. You were thinking. Thinking you can treat me like...like some...I don't know what." She pulled the wet towel back and he could see her tears. "This isn't working. We will move back into the shelter tonight. It's best—"

"No," he roared, coming up out of the chair. "You aren't leaving me." He picked her up and set her on the counter where sprinkles and icing was strewn about. When she started to get down, he simply stared at her. "I'm an idiot." He swore he heard her say she wouldn't argue with him about that, but he chose to ignore it. "I've been an idiot before about a woman and I lost my heart. She did things, said things that made me think I'd never give my heart to anyone again. Then your son came along and sat down beside me. So I—"

"And it's my fault too that you—"

"Hush, I'm not finished. He folds his cupcake wrappers, did you know that? And he is the neatest kid I've ever known. Then you come along and I figure out where he gets his compulsive tendencies and his smart mouth from. You, Heather, you are his mom."

"I'm well aware of being his mother. If you are finished, I'd like to gather my family and get out of your hair." She started to get down off the table. Alex stepped up to her and bracketed her there with his arms on either side of her. "Let me go."

"I fell in love with your grandda too. Fell in love with his odd way of getting around the story with a tale of nothing. And do you know what else?"

"You're making no sense. Let me down from here. I've work—"

"I fell in love with you too." He could see the shock in her eyes just before they became angry again. He loved that about her too. Her quick mind.

"You don't know what you're talking about. Let me down this minute. I have to make sure that Grandda has Jack so that we can move our things tonight."

"I have them both in my car. We're going to go to my mom's and have Thanksgiving dinner tomorrow. But tonight, I'm going to make love to you, slowly and all night."

Her eyes darkened and he watched her tongue wet her lush lips. He felt his cock harden at the thought of tasting her again and he moved slowly toward her mouth. Her sigh nearly had him throw her back on the table and take her there, but he was aware that they weren't in a place he could indulge in that right at the moment.

"Give me your mouth, Heather. Let me drink from you." Alex brushed his mouth over hers and moaned. "You taste like sugar to me, warm cookies and hot fires, of carnal thoughts and sex. I want you, Heather, right here right now."

He pulled her close and covered his mouth with his. Her hands encircled his neck and she opened beneath him. His tongue dove and took even as she wrapped her legs around his hips. Using his left hand, he pulled her body flush with his and felt her moan into his mouth. Pain ripped him away from her and had him stagger slightly. He wasn't sure what had happened until a voice behind him had him turning to protect Heather.

"You let him go this minute, Heather Colleen. You filthy slut. Right here where everyone can see you whore your ways on this man. Have you no decency?"

"Who the fuck are you? And what the fuck did you hit me for?" Alex saw her raise the cane up and knew that she was going to hit him again. He had just enough time to put his hand up before he thought the thing should hit him. But she was suddenly on the floor and Tom was standing over her.

"I knew that was you coming in here like you owned the place." Without taking his eyes from the woman on the floor, Tom made the introductions. "Alexander James, meet my daughter and Heather's mother, though I use that term because it wouldn't be proper to say what she's really been. This is Victoria Laird, the bitch who tossed her only child out onto the streets."

# Chapter 19

Heather tried not to think about what had happened. She glanced up at Alex again and dropped her head when she realized he was looking at her. She just wished the stupid doctor would come so she could go back and pack up. Alex cleared his throat and had her looking up at him.

"Come here, Heather. Come here and let me see you." His voice was husky and it did things to her system she wished she could control. "Heather?"

"I'm sure you can see me just fine from here." She flushed when she remembered he was only here because she'd come into his home. "I'm sorry about this. I didn't even know she knew where I was. I will try and pay for this hospital stay too."

Her mother had hit him hard enough that he needed stitches. The nurse said it would probably be around ten of them. She looked up at him when he laughed.

"Come here. Please." She looked up at him. "I want to hold you."

"Why?" But she got up and went to him anyway. "I don't understand you. My mother beats you with her cane and you end up in the hospital, and now you want to hold me. What do you think your mother will say about this?"

He pulled her onto the gurney with him and held her. "She will probably say that I should have ducked faster. Or paid attention to my surroundings instead of making love to a woman on a table top."

"You were not making love to me. And you won't either. I'm so sorry for all this." She started to pull away when the nurse came in.

"No. Don't go. I need you to stay. Please. Stay until my mom comes by." She was nearly ready to stay when the nurse spoke up.

"I'm sorry, Mr. James, she can't stay. She's not family. We've bent the rules enough to let her stay back here until now."

She started to turn away when Alex spoke again. "If you leave, I'll find you. I mean it, Heather. I will find you."

"I won't be hard to find. I've already told you where we're going. Goodbye, Mr. James. I'm sorry about everything."

"Damn it, Heather, get back here. Heather." She kept walking.

Heather told her grandda to gather their things at the house. He'd not been happy about it, but he said he would. Jack was less happy about leaving, but did what she'd asked him to do. She told him that Vickie wouldn't stop, wouldn't stop hurting those that they cared about.

It was bitterly cold out when she left the hospital. She had to walk to the shelter because her things, including her bus pass, were still at the bakery. She didn't know how she was going to get it back before Monday, but knew that Caroline would take care of it. If she still had a job.

Her mother had been there, kept playing in her mind. Her mother had said...poor Jack. She could still see the hurt on his face when her mother had called him a spawn of the devil.

"You should have gotten rid of him when I told you to. At the very least you should have drowned him when he was an infant. To think I thought you'd be smarter than this." Vickie had spewed her hatred of her and Jack relentlessly before the police arrived. Then she'd shut up.

"You don't know what the hell you're talking about. She's a great mother, and this boy loves her." Grandda had stood up to his daughter for all of ten minutes. Then he'd crumbled when she turned on him.

"You couldn't even save Mother, could you, old man? There she lay in her bed calling your name and you were out working. Couldn't be bothered to come home and be there when she died. Some judge of character you turned out to be." Vickie turned to Alex then. "And you. What do you think she's going to give you but some disease? She lured my poor husband to her bed then accused him of raping her."

"And the other girls he'd done the same thing to, I suppose they all lured him there as well? Is that the way it happened, or have you colored things to look the way you want to? I read the transcript of the trial. I know what happened in that bedroom. And it was just like she said it was." Alex took the cane from her that she still held in her hand like a weapon and broke it over his knee. "You raise a hand to any of them again and I'll hunt you down."

"You think to threaten me? Why, I have money. Money enough that would make you look like a pauper.

What do you do anyway? Run this little bakery? Make your little cakes? You haven't got a clue who I am." Her mother started to rise and Alex put his foot on her chest.

"I'm Alexander James and my family owns and operates the largest hotel business in the world. I know just who you are, Victoria Elizabeth Laird, only daughter to Thomas and Colleen Laird. You got your money the old fashioned way, through divorce and greed. Well, I've got news for you. I've got more money than you'll see in three life times."

Alex had shoved her back down and then dropped to the floor. Heather hadn't noticed that he'd been bleeding quite badly from the wound on his back. When he looked up at her, he smiled. "Stay with me for a bit longer, Heather. I might need to be sick and I want you there." Then he closed his eyes.

Her heart had broken then. He'd only wanted her there to clean up after him. She held him until they medics came and then went to the hospital with him. He'd woken in the ambulance and reached for her hand. She gave it to him and didn't say anything as he squeezed her too tight. Her mother was on her way to the station and her family was going back to the house.

She walked for a bit longer when she realized that she was near her old apartment building. There was nothing left of it; the bulldozers had already come in and knocked it all down. Her tears weren't so much for the loss as the memories they'd made there. And some of the things they'd never get back.

Pictures, for one. There weren't all that many because they'd never had the money to pay for a camera, but there had been a few. Jack's birth certificate was another thing she'd lost. Of course she could get another copy, but this one had been hers. There were the things he'd made her in his classes. The noodle-covered shoe box that held her few pieces of jewelry. The ornaments he'd made and they'd hung on the tiny artificial tree they'd gotten from the Goodwill they used every year. Her cook books that she'd picked up here and there at garage sales and tag sales. And the hundreds of other things she couldn't think of right now.

There were Christmas lights in the building next door. Lights that she knew that Jack would marvel over and want. She'd never had the money to spend on lights before, and she had wanted to do it this year. She'd been saving her change to do just that for him and now it was gone as well.

Steven Baxter had taken so much from her, so much that she'd never get back, but he'd given her one thing that she would gladly do it all over for and that was her son. Jack was her world and her life, and she didn't...couldn't think what she'd do without him. She turned and started walking toward the shelter again.

She saw Grandda first then Jack. They were both standing next to a large car and talking to a man Heather had never seen before. The closer she got, the more nervous she got until Jack saw her and started running toward her. Even as bad as things were, she still smiled when he hugged her.

"Mom, this is Mr. Stone. He said he was sent to pick us up. And we get to ride in this big limo." Jack was dragging her to the car and the man and woman standing there. "She's his wife, Mrs. Stone. And guess what? They are the mom and dad of Mr. Stone that I work for."

"Hello, Miss Laird. You have a wonderful family. I was wondering if we could persuade you to come along with us? Jared said that Alex needs you."

"Alex? What's wrong? My mother didn't come back, did she?" She looked at the woman then. "He sent you to fetch me back, didn't he?"

"Yes, I'm afraid he did. His mother is at the hospital with him now and we were sent to find you here. I must say he has quiet a temper, doesn't he? He is refusing treatment unless you come back to the hospital. The man was yelling at the doctor when we left." Mrs. Stone laughed. "I'm not sure who was more upset by his language, the doctor he was yelling at or his mom."

"Yes, he can be...colorful when the mood strikes him. I'm sorry to have wasted your time, Mr. and Mrs. Stone, but my family and I have other plans. We appreciate you coming here, but as you can see—"

"I was afraid you were going to say that. Well then, I guess I'll have to tell you the real reason we're here. Alex said you're pregnant and he told us to bring you to him so that he can make things right between you. Now, if you wouldn't mind—"

She cut Mr. Stone off. "I assure you, I'm not pregnant. I don't..." Heather looked down at her son who was staring at her with his mouth open. "I don't know what he's talking about. If you would be so kind as to just go back and tell him that I said leave me alone, then—"

"I can't do that. He told us what happened and I...well, I believe him. Alex hasn't ever lied to me before so I'm willing to bet he's not now." He opened the car door. "Please get inside, Miss Laird, and if this turns out to be a complete misunderstanding then I'll personally bring you back here myself."

Heather looked up at her grandda and could see that he was shocked as well. When he nodded at her, she felt as if the entire world was against her and went to the door. Jack scrambled in before her and Grandda got in the front.

"You're going to feel really bad when this turns out to be a bad joke, Mr. Stone. I believe Mr. James is a few crackers short of a picnic basket. You have to know this isn't right."

He nodded. "Maybe. But he said that the last time you had sex, the condom broke. As much as I think that's sharing a bit much, I can't let him not try and make a home for his child. Too many people don't care if they make a child, and even less should be raising one."

Heather could feel the tears threaten. "He wants his child then." She got in the car and ignored the man getting in behind her. Mrs. Stone got in beside Jack and talked to him in low tones. Heather turned away from the people in the car and stared out the window.

Heather tried to think about the last time they'd had sex. The sex part was easy to remember, but the part about the broken condom she had no idea. She wasn't sure how quickly they could tell if she was pregnant or not, but she was pretty sure that they wouldn't be able to tell from two days ago. But it would be her luck that he was correct and she was now carrying another man's child.

She glanced over at Jack. She wondered what he thought of his mother being pregnant, or for that matter, her grandda. He'd gotten in the front of the car for a reason she was sure. He was ashamed of her. Well, she thought as she turned back to the window, she was as well. When the car slid to a smooth stop, she didn't even wait for the driver to come around, but got out and went into the emergency room.

"Thank goodness," Mrs. James said as soon as she saw her. "You scared us all leaving like that. Come on, he needs to see you."

She let herself be lead to another part of the department. There was a door on this area and once it was open, Heather could hear him yelling at someone. She moved the curtain out of the way and stood there until he turned to look at her.

~~~

Alex knew the moment he saw her she was mad. Well, he'd fix that soon enough now that she was here. He didn't notice when everyone left the room. He could only stare at her.

"I'm glad you came back. I needed you here with me." She moved to the chair without a word and sat there. "Heather, you might be having my baby. I can't let you live in the shelter knowing that."

It had been a long shot using that. Jared had used the same thing on Wills when she wouldn't marry him too. He didn't like to do it, but he needed her. He started to move off the bed when the doctor came in.

"Ah, there you are. You've caused us quite a stir leaving like you did." Heather nodded, but still didn't speak. "Are you ready now, Alex? I do have other patients."

"Yes, I'm ready. Heather, will you come here and hold me?" She stood and he thought she was going to leave again when she looked at the door. "Heather?"

She walked to the side of the bed and took his hand. Hers was cold and he wondered what she'd been doing. Before he could ask, his mom walked in with Jack.

"He wanted to see you for just a minute. I couldn't turn him down." Heather put her arm around Jack when he stood close to her as his mom continued. "His grandpa Tom said to tell you he'd see you at the house. He said that hospitals make him nervous and that he'd rather not be here."

"Mr. Alex, is mom really going to have a baby?" Alex glanced up at Heather at Jack's question.

"We'll have to wait and see, buddy. There are tests we'd have to have run to make sure. But it could be. Heather, are you all right?" Alex thought she looked pale, but she only shook her head. "Please speak to me."

"Jack, could you please sit quietly for me? Mr. James needs to be stitched up. I don't think it will take much longer." Jack did as his mother said. Neither of them looked all that happy about this.

Well, Alex thought, he wasn't really happy about it either. He wanted to make a life with this woman and her son and he didn't like resorting to blackmail to get her to listen to him. He nodded at the doctor when he cleared his throat again. His mom sat next to Jack and held his hand. Heather stared at the wall and not at him.

The Novocain numbed the area and he could feel the thread going in and out of his skin. The longer she stood there holding his hand and ignoring him, the madder he got. By the time the doctor said he was finished, Alex was royally pissed.

"Mom, could you take Jack to the lobby for a minute? I think Heather and I have something to say to each other." Alex sat up and watched as his mom stood. Jack walked to his mother and held her hand.

"Go ahead, son. I'll be out soon. I'll be all right here." Heather kissed her son and he left the room.

"He probably thinks I'm going to beat you." Alex nearly said that she deserved it too, but didn't. "Are you going to speak to me?"

"Would it matter what I say? You seemed to have it all worked out. Why don't you tell me your plans for your child?" She sat down hard and he almost felt sorry for the chair. "Well, tell me what the great and powerful Alexander James has up his sleeve."

"You don't need to be snarky about it. I was going to tell you about the condom yesterday, but you left for work. How the hell was I supposed to know you'd been released to go back?" He stood up and put on the clean shirt his mom had brought him. "I won't have you raising my child in a shelter."

He knew the moment he'd said it that it had come out all wrong. He turned back to her to see the tears on her cheeks and nearly went to her when she held up her hand to stop him. He wondered if he'd ever get it right with her.

"I had no intentions of living in a shelter for the rest of my life. I have plans as well. And none of them include having another child. Ever. I can't have a baby. I don't have the resources to do this right now." She stood and started pacing. "I suppose you'll want to keep tabs on me. I can live with that. I won't do anything to hurt your baby. I don't know how you feel about the clinic, but that's all I can afford righ—"

"You're going to marry me, Heather. As soon as it can be arranged. I want my child to have my name and marrying me will make sure of that." She stopped pacing and stared at him before she threw back her head and laughed. "What the hell is so funny?"

"You want me to marry you because I might be pregnant? No, I don't think so. If I am pregnant then I will sign whatever you want that gives you the baby, but I won't marry you."

"We'll just see about that."

# Chapter 20

Heather looked down at her borrowed dress and started to cry again. She was getting married in ten minutes and there wasn't a damned thing she could do about it. She walked over to the window in the bedroom she'd been assigned when she'd been brought to the James' house the day before yesterday.

Alex had played her badly...or well, she supposed. He'd used Jack as a way to get around her. He'd all but promised to give him all his worldly possessions for her to marry him. And now Jack was going to get to go to the best college and not have to worry about working to do it. He'd have money to spend and a car to drive when he was ready. He'd have it all. And all his mom had to do was to sell herself on a permanent basis to his provider.

She looked up when her grandda entered the room. "They're ready for you, honey. Are you ready?"

He looked so good in his suit and tie she couldn't help but to fuss over it. She smiled at him through her tears, hoping he'd think they were happy tears and not sad ones. He grinned down at her.

"Your old man can clean up with the best of them, can't he? You should see Jack in his finery." He frowned then. "Have you figured out what is wrong with him?"

Jack had been quiet since they'd arrived here on Thanksgiving morning. He'd not eaten much, nor had he said much to anyone. At nine o'clock, he'd gone to bed, even turning down a chance to play in the garage with some power tools that Alex's dad had offered to let him use.

"No. You think he is unhappy with Mr. James about something?" He winced when she called Alex by the "mister" part again.

"He ain't gonna be none too happy with you if you don't start calling him Alex like he said. A wife doesn't call her husband Mr."

A wife didn't have to be coerced into marriage either, but she let it go. "I'll talk to him after the...the ceremony."

He grabbed her arms when she made to step away. "Are you going to be happy with him, Heather? I won't have you sad on your wedding day. If you don't think this will work out, then I'll make sure you and that baby are well taken care of."

She felt tears again. "I'm fine, Grandda. Really, this is the best solution for everyone. And Jack will be able to get all the chances I would never have been able to give him."

She'd told him everything, including the contract she'd signed with Alex. She would be his wife in all ways—the only way he'd let her, and Jack would get a great education and a father figure. She would be well provided for as well, she just didn't know what that would be.

They were married in the large family room. Heather thought they could just go to the Justice of the Peace, but

Mrs. James had vetoed that idea immediately. Wills had leant her the dress she had on and even the shoes. Heather didn't care so long as it was over soon.

The room had been decorated with flowers; most of them had been brought in just this morning. Heather had watched the men bring them in by the armloads. She watched people start arriving as soon as the vans left and Heather wondered what they were thinking of a wedding being planned and executed in such a short amount of time. But for the most part, she'd stayed out of the way and left the details up to those that had the money.

When the minister had told them they could kiss, she hoped that Alex would simply kiss her on the cheek and be done with it. She turned her head to offer it to him when he wrapped his arm around her and pulled her close. She knew the moment he brushed his mouth over hers that he was going to kiss her, really kiss her. It took her several seconds after he finally let her up for air to realize that everyone was clapping. She didn't say anything when people started slapping him on the back and hugging her to them.

As soon as they were seated to eat the light dinner, Alex pulled her close. "You should really try to enjoy yourself. Mom went to a great deal of trouble to make this day special for you."

"Special for you, don't you mean? I'm doing the best I can. I don't know any of these people, including your parents. Now you got what you wanted, leave me alone."

He pulled her to him for a hard kiss. He had meant to punish her, she was sure, but all she could do was feel the heat of the kiss and his body close to hers. When she pulled away, it was all she could do not to whimper and beg him to do it again.

"You could be happy if you let yourself. I only want what is best for you. I'm in love with you and I want us to be happy."

She turned away from him before he saw the hurt. She wasn't even sure anymore what she was hurt about, but her heart did ache. She saw her son then and he smiled at her. She didn't think he was any happier than she was.

~~~

Candace watched the couple leave for their honeymoon. It really wasn't going to be much more than a night in the bridal suite at one of their hotels. She could almost feel sorry for Heather if she wasn't sure the girl loved Alexander. She started up for bed when she noticed the light on in the kitchen. She went in there to tell her husband to put the cake away and go to bed when she saw Jack sitting there.

She noticed that he was using one of Alex's laptops and wondered if she should get him one for Christmas. He was her grandson now and she couldn't wait to spoil him. But she was worried about him being so sad.

"I was just coming in to have a bowl of ice cream. Would you like to join me?" She noticed that he closed the lid on the computer before she could see what he was doing. "I have chocolate and strawberry. Which do you prefer?"

"I'm not supposed to have sweets. Mom said that dental work is expensive and sweets can make you fat." He eyed the dessert longingly. "Besides, I don't think I've ever had any kind but vanilla."

"Well I don't think one bowl will hurt you too much. We'll make sure you brush your teeth extra hard to be sure to get them clean." She got down two bowls. "Are you allergic to chocolate or strawberry, Jack? I should have asked your mom before she left."

"No, ma'am. I just don't care for strawberries and my mom is allergic to chocolate. She can touch it but not eat it, makes her throw up." He looked at the dark, rich ice cream she had spooned into her bowl. "But I'm not. If I brush really well then I don't think she'll mind too much."

They ate their dessert in silence for a few minutes. Jack seemed to eat his in a pattern and when she watched him, she could see that he was dividing it up into portions before he took a bite. She remembered Alex telling them that he was a compulsive person and now she could see it.

"What are you doing on the computer?" He looked up at her, alarmed. "You're not on one of those adult sites, are you, Jack? Your mother would kill me if you were."

"No," he nearly shouted at her. "No, ma'am. I was looking…I was just wondering about something. About schools and stuff."

She could tell that he was hiding something and she liked to pride herself on knowing what her children were about before they knew she did. She nodded to him, trying to think of a way to get it out of him. "What sort of schools? I know you'll be applying to colleges in a few years. I'm pretty sure that as smart as you are, you'll be able to get into any one you want. Is that what you're looking into?"

"No, ma'am." He started playing with his ice cream before he answered. "I was looking at the kind of school people send their kids off to when they have a baby coming in the house."

She was stunned. He thought…she wasn't sure what he thought, but if he was thinking Alex would send him…Then it hit her.

"You think because if your mom is pregnant that Alex will want to keep his own child close and send you away." The tears in his eyes said it all. "Oh honey, that's not going to happen. Alex loves you. He's not going to want to send you away. And I'm pretty sure your mother will hurt him if he tried."

"But I'm a bastard. Nobody wants a bastard around. I'm not his kid and he'll love the new baby so much he'll not want me around. It happened to some of my friends at school. Every time their moms got married, they'd have to change schools."

"First of all, who told you that you were a bastard? You are no such a thing. You're a bright, loving little boy who is much too smart to believe that because your mom didn't marry your father that makes you something you're not."

"But Vickie said —" he started.

"Vickie is full of shit." He grinned at her. "I see you agree. Well listen here, kid, you're my grandson now and I'm the one who will be kicking some serious ass if she tries to tell you that again. Now here's something else you should know. Your mother isn't happy."

"She looked so sad when she left with Mr. Alex. Did she not want to marry him or something?"

"I don't think your mom believes anyone could love her but you and your grandpa Tom. She thinks that Alex is only marrying her because she might be pregnant."

Jack looked down at his bowl again. "Isn't he? Mom told me that she didn't even know she was pregnant yet but she was providing for me anyway. I'm not sure what she means, but she seemed really sad about it."

"I think she loves Alex, but is afraid to tell even herself. She thinks what her mother said is true. That Alex only wants her for one thing."

"Sex." Candace was a little surprised, but didn't comment. He was a smart kid. "He kisses her all the time and she seems to like it when he does. I don't get it, seems kind of messy and nasty to me."

Candace laughed. "I'm sure it does when you're nine. But you'll change your tune soon enough. I hope I'm around when you do."

They finished their treat and were cleaning up the kitchen when Edgar came in. He fussed at them for not having him in for ice cream and sat down at the table to pout. Jack opened the laptop again.

"Mr. James, do you know what this is doing here?" Jack turned the computer to show him. Candace looked over their shoulder.

"I don't know what I'm looking at, son. And you can call me Grandda if you want, or Edgar. I wouldn't mind the first, but I'll take the second."

Candace grinned at her husband. "Please, Jack, call us Grandma and Grandpa. We've been waiting forever for someone to call us that."

Jack flushed and nodded then pointed to the icon on the computer. "This is a spywear program. It's used so that someone can look into someone else's computer." He pointed at another one. "This one is to guard this computer. See, it's sort of like a two-way mirror. This computer can see in, but nobody can see back."

Candace closed the computer for a second then opened it back up. "I think this was Brick's computer. Alex brought it here when he came by the other day. Do you think this has anything to do with his death?" she asked her husband, completely forgetting the little boy for a moment.

Candace looked at Jack when he stood. "Somebody died? Why? Oh gosh, is it because of the money?"

"Money? What do you know, Jack? You have to tell us everything." Candace looked at her husband and nodded. "I'll make us something to eat. Jack, you start talking, honey."

Candace debated for all of ten seconds on whether or not to call Alex and Heather back. But she decided she'd listen first then call if it was necessary. Fear gripped her heart, but she told herself that they had the best security system in the world and would keep this little boy safe.

# Chapter 21

Alex was nervous. He paced around the hotel room waiting on Heather to come out of the bathroom for — he looked at his watch and grinned — all of five minutes now. He looked at the bed and thought about the two of them there. His cock was already aching and if he kept this up, as soon as she walked through the door he was going to pounce on her. When he heard the lock disengage, he turned to see her.

She was beautiful, so beautiful that his breath caught. Her hair was down now and he hadn't realized how long it was. Her cheeks were flushed and he had a moment to realize she was just as nervous as he was. But it was her clothes that had him swallow several times before he trusted himself to speak.

The sheer pink material left very little to the imagination. The tiny ribbons at her shoulders held up the triangle of lace that was tight across her breasts; her nipples stood hard out from it. There was another ribbon at the center and that was all that held it on her. It opened the rest of the way. The panties, if that was what one would call a small bit of lace of the same shade of pink, covered just her mound and nothing else. More ribbon tied at her hips and he wondered if he would die right now if she turned around.

"Your sister gave it to me. She said it was a wedding present to you. I didn't understand that until you looked at me. Do you like it?" She sounded so unsure that he looked up at her face.

"Yes. I love it. You look…Christ, Heather you take my breath away. I'm almost afraid to ask you to turn around. Is there much of it back there?"

She grinned and turned. "I feel like I'm sexy. I know that sounds stupid, it's just a nightie, but—"

"You do look sexy, you *are* sexy. I'm not going to last." He was right about the back. The ribbons holding it together at her hips slid between her cheeks and disappeared. He couldn't wait to peel it from her. Her back was covered, but that wasn't really right either. He could see every inch of her including the tattoo at her spine.

He started toward her slowly. He wanted to push her against the wall and take her now, but this was her wedding night, their wedding night, and he wanted it to be special. He thought maybe if he didn't take his pants off he might last another whole ten seconds. Grinning, he lifted her chin with his finger, not touching her anywhere else.

He'd meant to only touch his lips to hers, but the moment he did, she moaned and he was lost. Her mouth opened under his and her tongue slid along his in a dance that he'd never felt before. Pulling back slightly, he looked down at her.

"I decided to make the best of this." She flushed as she tried to look away. "I know you want me and I want you. There isn't any reason we can't enjoy ourselves, is there?"

"No. No, there isn't. But, Heather, I do love you. I know you find that hard to believe, but I do. I want to make you happy."

She pulled away from him and walked to the window. "I know you say that, but you don't know me. I mean, you know what everyone has told you, but all we've done since we met is fight. I don't know how you can…you can't love someone like me."

He walked toward the ice bucket and the champagne his parents had had put in the room for them. He opened it with a pop and poured them both a glass. Walking toward her, he answered her unspoken question.

"I don't believe anything your mother told me. None of it. My sister Wills told me what you told her that day. She said she fell in love with you too by the way. And Wills is the hardest person I know in making friends." He handed her the fluted glass. "If I could find Baxter, I'd murder him myself after I thanked him."

She turned to look at him. "Thank him? Whatever for? He was a slimy dickhead who preyed on young women."

"I'm glad to hear you say that. But I'd thank him for Jack. He's a wonderful kid and I want to adopt him. But for now…" He took the glass from her when she emptied it. "For now, we'll forget all the others and concentrate on getting you out of this piece of froth. Would you like me to peel if from you an inch at a time, or tear it from you and ravage you? I'm up for either right now."

He'd meant it to be glib, but he knew when he looked at her he'd failed. He touched his finger down her cheek and wiped the tear away. He didn't want her to cry, but could almost understand why she did. She'd had a very difficult life and he so desperately wanted to make it better for her.

He kissed her gently then took the ribbon on her shoulder into his mouth. As she watched him, he pulled it back until it was untied. Then he did the same to the other. A deep breath would have had the lace fall from her. He lowered his head to her breast and laved it, material and all, until her nipple was straining against the wet. Slowly, he ran his hand up her ribs to cup her breast from beneath. When he felt her shudder, he grabbed the top of the nightie with his teeth and pulled it away.

"You have the most luscious breasts. And your nipples are perfect. The dusky rose color contrasts wonderfully with your pale skin. When it puckers like it is now, I want to suckle hard on it until you come." Her moan moved through his veins like molten lava and made him want more.

"When you...when you touch me like this, I can feel my privates swell. I can feel myself getting wetter." She blushed a bright red and he found himself wanting to see it more. He took her nipple into his mouth and nipped at the tip just enough to have her surge to him. He suckled hard as he slid his hand to her mound and into the tiny triangle at her pussy. She wasn't wet, she was soaking.

"Say it, Heather. Tell me how wet your pussy is. Tell me what you want and call it your pussy." Her blush deepened and he could feel her stiffen. Taking her breast into his palm, he tugged on her nipple and moved to the other side. "Do you want to come. Do you want to come now?"

"Yes. Yes, that's what I want, but...shouldn't we be in the bed?" She started to pull back and he stilled her with his free hand. "Alex?"

"No. I'm going to lick your pussy. Lick you until you come in my mouth. I want to drink you before I fuck you. Tell me that's what you want, Heather. Say it." He found he needed to hear her say it, needed her to tell him that she wanted him as much as he did her. He lowered his hand back to her mound and moved his finger just over her nether lips, not touching her clit. She started to ride his fingers when he pulled back. "Say it." He looked down at her now. Her eyes were dark, darker than he'd ever seen them. Her bare breast filled his palm and he rubbed his thumb roughly over the tip. Her eyes fluttered. His cock was hurting, aching to be free so that he could fill her.

"I want you to fuck me, Alex. I want you to suck on my pussy until I come. Please, please take me. I need to come." Her words nearly undid him. Her voice, husky with need, tore at his control until he thought he'd die.

Dropping to his knees, he took the strings in his fingers and pulled them loose while she watched. Sliding his hands up her thighs, he pulled her legs farther apart, gathered the cream on her, and took it to his mouth.

"Hummm, delicious. Creamy and hot. I'm going to enjoy having this all for myself."

Opening her lips, he could see she was indeed swollen. Her clit was red and puffy, full and tempting. He knew she was close and wanted to give her a short release before he enjoyed her. Taking her hard nubbin into his mouth, he fucked her with his tongue as he filled her with his finger. She came immediately.

Her juices poured from her. Lapping and sucking, he gathered every drop on his tongue and savored her. She was his. Now and forever, she was his. Making her come once more, he could feel her legs beginning to tremble. Afraid she would fall, he stood, picked her up, and laid her on the bed.

"Christ, you taste good. But I need to be inside of—" His mind spun out of control when she spread her legs and slid her finger deep into her pussy. He watched as she moved her finger around her clit then deep inside over and over. Her moans grew louder as her fingers went faster.

"Alex, please. Hurry. Please?" He would wonder later if he stripped his clothes off or they just disappeared. Because he was suddenly naked and standing over her, his cock in his fist and his own cream dripping from the tip.

When she sat up and reached for him, he knew that if she touched him, he'd come. He was barely holding on now. When he reached for a condom, he stopped and looked down at her. "I want to fill you with my seed, Heather. I want to see you grow large with my child, our child. Now, tonight, I want to be inside of you deep, deep enough to touch your womb and fill you."

Her breath hitched and she nodded. He lay on the bed and kissed her as he settled between her thighs. Her heat, her wetness, made his cock jerk. His need for her was overwhelming.

Alex took her nipple into his mouth and suckled as he slid into her. Her body gripped him tight and rippled along his cock until he had to pause or come. Stilling in her body, he held himself up on his elbows as he tried to calm himself.

But she had other ideas. With a shift of her body, he was buried deep and as she grabbed his shoulders, he rocked hard into her. His control was nearly gone.

"I feel you, feel you so deep in me. You're so thick, hot and thick. Please, fuck me, Alex. Please."

He rocked again, this time with more power than finesse. "Heather, I'm trying to make this last. You're killing me, baby. If you move again, I'm—"

She did and the nails holding onto his control snapped. He took her hard, took her fast, and simply took. She didn't back off, but met him stroke for stroke. When he felt her sheath grab him, nearly strangle him with her climax, Alex didn't just tumble after her. He went roaring over the cliff and didn't look back.

~~~

Heather woke and had a sudden fright when she couldn't figure out where she was. Then the night before came back at her and she smiled. Stretching, she felt muscles protest, ones she wasn't even aware she had until then. But it was a good feeling, one of being relaxed and well used. She started to roll to her side when an arm fell across her waist.

Alex. They'd had sex, incredible sex, and he'd fallen atop of her and both of them went to sleep. Getting out of the big bed, she went to the bathroom and closed the door. She looked in the mirror when she turned the light on and didn't recognize the woman staring back at her. This woman looked happy, sated of course, but more. More of what she didn't want to think about so she finished up and went back to the bed.

He took up most of the bed, she noticed, and wondered if he'd even miss her if she left. But being his wife now, she knew that was no longer an option. Plus, they'd had unprotected sex, sex to create a child. She sat down hard on the floor. What the hell had she been thinking?

Putting her hand on her flat belly, she wondered if one was already growing there. A baby changed...she wasn't sure now that this was such a good idea. Looking at the man she'd pledged to, she wondered if he'd think the same thing in the light of the day.

His face calmed her. Just looking at him sleep, his whole body lax in slumber, she felt she had made the right decision. He was a good man, a great man, she supposed. She knew so very little about him other than what his sister had told him at Thanksgiving.

Heather knew he'd been married before. His wife had died carrying another man's child. Willow had told her that Alex had been too young to realize what his parents had told him was true about her; he'd been in love. When she died, it had taken a great deal out of Alex and they all thought he'd never get it back.

Resting her chin on her fist, she moved closer to the bed. His jaw was covered in dark whiskers and she wondered if they were soft. Touching her finger to the fur, she realized they were hard and prickly. His lips were full, swollen slightly from last night. Shifting slightly, she remembered him taking her into his mouth and making her come. She looked down at his bare ass and wondered how hard it would be to roll him over. She wanted to get a good look at him was all, she told herself, and stood up.

Touching her fingers to his hip, he shifted. When touching him again only made him more in the center of the bed, she ran her hand up his thigh in much the way he'd done to her. His moan made her jerk her hand back and watch as he rolled to his side. Perfect. She could get a good look at his…form while he was still asleep.

His cock lay flaccid, though still large, and she found her mouth water at the sight of him. She touched the very tip of him and then ran her finger around the large head. He rolled to his back with another moan. His cock jerked now and Heather wanted to taste him in the worst way. Shifting to the bed, she moved his legs open and settled herself between them. She thought she could simply take him in her mouth and he'd never be the wiser. Leaning down, she licked her tongue along the thick vein along the length of him. He hardened even as she swirled her tongue over his dark head.

Need overpowered her curiosity. Adjusting herself so that she could move over him, she took him into her mouth. His cock grew in her mouth, hardened and lengthened until she had to swallow or be gagged. He tasted delicious and warm and the more she took of him into her, the hotter he became.

His hand tangled in her hair and she looked up; his eyes were still closed but his face looked to be in pain. Hungry for him, she bobbed up and down over him as she wrapped her hand around him. He rocked into her mouth hard, his hips coming up off the bed as he tried to go deeper. She knew the moment he woke. His breath hissed out and he looked down at her.

"Christ, woman, have mercy. Please." She let him go, but didn't move away from her position. "Don't stop. If you do, I won't be responsible for what I do to you."

"Tell me how to please you. I want to do this." She thought his eyes rolled to the back of his head, but as he sat up on his elbows, she thought he looked like he wanted to eat her alive.

"Cup my balls, gently. That's it. Christ, Heather, your mouth feels wonderful." She cupped his balls in her hand and rolled them between her fingers. His cock jerked again. Wrapping his hand around his shaft, he guided it to her mouth and she licked him.

"Take me in your mouth like you were. Take me as deep as you can and—yes," he hissed at her. "That's it. Baby, I'm going to come down your throat if you keep that up. When you feel my cock at the back of your throat, swallow and—mother fuck, I'm coming."

The first splash of his cum gagged her, but she swallowed hard and felt it slide. As her mouth filled with his hot juices, she began moving her hand up and down him. His hand at her head held her still, but she didn't stop. Over and over she let him fuck her mouth until she felt him pull her away. Her body was on fire. She needed relief now.

"Come here. Ride me. I want you to ride me." His voice sounded like he'd been straining it. And it moved over her body like a caress. But she didn't know what he meant.

"Straddle me, your pussy over my cock." She crawled up until she was over him. When he pulled her down and took her mouth, she was sure he could taste him on her tongue and her pussy gushed more.

With her hips up, she felt him take his cock in his hand and rub it over her clit. Pushing down onto him, she moaned when he slid inside. He pushed, sitting her up, and she felt him deep, his cock beneath her, inside of her.

With his hands on her hips, he showed her how to move. Slowly at first, she began to see the advantages of riding. Moving more, she began to enjoy herself as she threw back her head. Rolling her hips over his, she felt her body come alive. Lifting her breasts, she began to roll her nipples and looked down at Alex when he covered her hands with his.

"Come for me. Come now." Her climax gripped her then spiraled out. Stars danced behind her eyelids and a scream erupted from her throat. Even as Alex rolled her to her back and began slamming into her, she felt another climax rip through her. Over and over her body tightened only to be torn open with a new harder zenith. When Alex went rigid over her and then roared out his own release, Heather felt herself slide into sleep, her body trembling with exhaustion.

# Chapter 22

Mik watched the men and women go in and out of the house. He wanted Alexander, not these idiots who were redoing the house. It was early on Monday morning and he'd already had to go and have a meeting with the two fools he'd sent here to find him. Meeting, he thought with a laugh. Hardly, more like a…well, more like a gun versus head kind of thing.

He was almost sorry to have had to kill the older one. But leaving witnesses, even ones as helpful as he had been, would be a mistake. He was sitting in the car they'd driven here from New York and wondered, not for the first time since he'd gotten in, how anyone could live like this.

The car was a dump. Not only were there stains on the seat that he didn't want to think about, but there was enough empty fast food trash that he was sure they could fill a land fill. The clothes in the backseat smelled like they'd been pissed on and he was sure that the nasty underwear had shit in them. He didn't clean it out because he didn't want to leave any DNA around for someone to find and start asking questions. It was his plan to leave the car near the bodies and just simply walk away. The car he had rented when he'd arrived had been here twice and he wanted to make sure that no one took notice.

Mik sat up when the limo pulled up in the drive. He was surprised when the gate closed behind it, but not overly worried. He'd been smart enough to snag a gate opener while he'd been here a few nights ago. It was amazing the things people left out when they thought they had locked the doors behind them. He wasn't sure who got out of the stretch, but he had an idea that the master of the house was finally home. He started up the car and went back to the house he'd had the idiots rent the day he'd arrived. Glad for the cold, he went into the house by the back door to avoid the mess that had been made in the front. Going to his small set up, he pulled up the small cameras he'd planted throughout the house.

*Ah, there we are.* He gave a chuckle. Going through the house was his Alexander, looking at what work had been done while he'd been away. Mik watched as he was joined by a beautiful woman, he thought perhaps his sister, and then an older man. Mik wished that he'd had sound, but there simply wasn't enough time for that.

He watched until he grew bored. How many times could a man go into a room and look around and see the same thing? Going to the house phone, Mik ordered a pizza and had it delivered. When he returned, they were all in the kitchen at the James house and the woman was cooking.

Potatoes were wrapped up in foil and then steaks, thick and juicy, were laid out on the counter. Pepper was coarsely ground over them then massaged into the meat. Mik found his mouth watered as the steaks were then put into a bowl and a bottle of something was poured over them. Then the woman took out the fixings for a salad — lettuce and tomatoes, peppers and onions. He recognized feta cheese and chickpeas along with cucumbers and fresh mozzarella. But what had him sit up and look closer was the dressing, homemade with extra virgin olive oil and wine. He thought that he'd died and gone to culinary heaven when she pulled out long loaves of crusty bread, made croutons, and tossed them in the oil before putting them in the oven.

Then Alexander came in the room and spoke to the woman. The closer he got to her, the woman backed up. He could see the lust on Alexander's face, the need for her. Even without the sound, he knew that he was telling the woman what he wanted, perhaps what he was going to do to her.

The kiss they shared was hot, steamy. Alexander molded the woman to his body and pressed her against the counter. Mik felt his own cock harden as he watched the two of them. Her leg lifted, skimming down Alexander's leg even as he lifted her up and sat her on the countertop. When both her legs wrapped around him, Mik rubbed his cock through his trousers. Aching, he pulled open his pants and took out his cock. Stroking himself, he watched as Alexander lifted her top and took her breast into his mouth. They were large and heavy and even through the bra he could see that she would fill his hands.

Mik shouted when Alexander backed away. His own cock straining for more, he screamed at the screen and waited for Alexander to continue. When the woman smiled at her would-be lover and pulled her shirt back into place, Mik stood and kicked trash around the room.

Pissed more than he'd ever been, he cursed the two of them for not giving him his due.

By the time the pizza arrived, Mik had worked himself into a full anger. He wanted to take it out on the man who'd come to the door, but knew that if he did that he'd be leaving more bodies and he wasn't close to being done here yet. Paying the man and leaving him no tip, Mik went into the little office and watched as they all enjoyed their steak dinner with baked potatoes and fresh salad while he dined on greasy cheese pizza and warm beer. Mik was going to make them pay for this. As soon as he got Alexander back where he belonged, he was going to make him pay for every injustice that Mik had had to endure.

~~~

Alexander didn't look at the camera, but continued on as if nothing was out of the ordinary. Jack had been able to tell them where every camera was because of the remote put on Brick's computer. They'd gone over the house to see where they were and had set up the plan accordingly. They were now sitting around the table trying to enjoy the steak dinner that Heather had fixed for them. His parents were there, as well as Tom, Jared, and Willow.

Alex hadn't wanted Wills there. Hell, he didn't want any of them there, but especially his sister. He was worried about her and the baby. Looking over at Jared, he figured he would keep her safe. Alex knew just how the man felt when he looked over at his own wife.

Wife. He still marveled at the fact that she was his. He had yet to convince her that he loved her, loved her more than life itself, but he would. He picked up her hand and kissed it. Soon, he thought. Soon she'd believe him. Then there was Jack.

The boy was undoubtedly brilliant. He'd found the program on Brick's computer in less than an hour and Alex had been looking at it for two days. He smiled when he thought of his face when Alex had told him how proud he was of him. He'd gotten red-faced and changed the subject. He was much like his mom in that neither of them seemed used to compliments and wasn't sure how to take them. That too, Alex thought, was going to change.

He realized that his dad was speaking to him and flushed when he laughed. "I was asking about tomorrow. Are you all set?"

Alex looked over at his sister. "Don't even say it." She answered his look. "I'm not leaving. This guy killed a friend of mine too and he is so not going to get away with it."

"I didn't say anything, but I'm going to say this again since you mentioned it. Stay away from him, Wills. I won't have you hurt over this. He's after me and we're going to play this like we were told. Understand?"

Wills looked at Heather. "He loves me, that's why he nags. Wait until you're huge with a kid and he starts ordering you around."

"He already does." Heather ginned. "Why do you think we fight all the time? I swear he's a bigger bully than that little boy in Jack's class. What was his name, honey?"

Alex looked at Jack and wondered if now was a good time to bring up the subject of schools. Alex's mom had told him what Jack had thought and wanted to clear that up before much longer. He also wanted to take the boy aside and talk to him about becoming his father. Heather said it was up to Jack and while she wanted the best for him, she felt Jack was a mature enough boy to know what he wanted.

"Peter Dunlap. He was older than me by a whole year and he would get mad at me and bloody my nose because I messed up the grading scale. He said I cheated. I didn't cheat. I studied. Why would someone get mad at me because I studied?" Jack seemed more upset that this older boy would call him a cheater than he'd been about the bloodied nose.

"I knew a Dunlap when I was in school," Jared said. "He was a dweeb. I think he was considered a bully as well. I wonder if he's his father. Christ, wouldn't...I mean darn, wouldn't that be funny?"

Alex laughed when Jared flushed. Candace James could cuss like a sailor when the mood struck, but she demanded that her children never do it in front of her. He'd heard her berate his father for ten minutes when he'd said "fuck" once then two days later had called the paperboy who'd thrown her newspaper in the bushes three days in a row a little "fuck-tard." He loved her to distraction.

"His dad is a dweeb," Jack told him. "His name is Richard Carter Dunlap. He says it like he's saying a prayer or something. I think he believes we should throw rose petals on the floor at open house when his dad comes in the room."

Everyone burst out laughing and Jared said he'd look it up when he got home and let him know. He couldn't remember the name, but he never forgot a fight. Jared slid right into the conversation they'd had earlier.

"Hey, Jack, now that you're going to be living here, Wills and I wanted to know if you'd like a pup? Come and It had a litter a few weeks back and we have two males and a female left. They're beautiful puppies. You could have your pick."

"You have dogs named Come and It? That's goofy. Why would you name them that?" Jack flushed. "I mean...I'm sorry, sir. I didn't mean to make fun of your dogs."

Wills rubbed Jack's head affectionately. "Don't worry about it. They do have weird names, but I didn't name them. I took them from this couple who didn't realize they'd get so big. Their real names are Damn it and Come Here."

Jack looked at her incredulously. "You're serious? Someone named your dogs Come Here Damn It?" Wills nodded. Jack looked at him. "Mr. Alex, is that the truth?"

"Yes, son, I'm afraid it is." He waited for a few seconds before he continued. "You could name your dog Right Now, that way when they play together you can yell, 'Come here damn it right now,' and they'll come running."

They all laughed and the tension was broken about Mik. But when Jack found him after dinner and asked to speak to him privately before he was supposed to be in bed, Alex was nervous. He wanted this kid to love him as much as he did him. They met in the yard where there didn't seem to be any cameras.

"Are you going to send me away, Mr. Alex? I know that I'm not your kid, but my mom needs me. And we've never been apart before. Plus, there's my grandpa Tom. He would miss me and I'd hate for him to need me and I'd be too far away for him when he needed me. I know I'm not—"

"Jack, I'm not going to send you away. I'd miss you too." Alex watched the boy crumple to the ground. "Are you all right? Christ, kid, don't scare me like that."

"I thought you'd want to get rid of me with Mom going to have your own baby and all. I was so afraid. Then when you said I could have a puppy, I thought maybe you'd let me come home sometime. Mr. Alex, thank you. I promise I won't give you any trouble. Ever."

Alex sat on the cold ground next to Jack. Neither of them said anything for a few minutes. Each seemed to be lost in thought. When Alex looked over at him, Jack was watching the stars.

"Your mom and I are going to have children, you understand that, right?" Jack nodded. "Good. I want to have lots, but we'll play that part by ear, I guess. They'll be called James as their surname, like mine and your mom's."

"Because you're married. Grandpa Tom said that I'd be a Laird because you weren't married to mom when I was born." Jack looked up at him then back to the ground. "I wish you had been. Mom wouldn't have had to work so hard if you had been."

Alex had no answer to that. He wished he'd been there for her as well. He took a deep breath before going on. "I would hate to have you the odd man out. So I was thinking, if you want, we can call you James too."

"I guess that would be okay. I like the name James. People could call me JJ then instead of Jackie-O. I'm not a girl."

Alex had to bite his cheek to keep from laughing at Jack's tone. He sounded so indignant about being called a girl. Not that he could blame him.

"Of course," Jack said slowly, "you could just adopt me then I'd really be Jack Thomas James instead of just calling me that."

Alex did laugh then. "That's a wonderful idea. I don't know why we didn't think of that. I take it you wouldn't mind being my son then."

"Oh no, sir. Not at all. Your mom and dad said I could call them Grandma and Grandpa—I haven't yet," he hurriedly explained. "I wanted to ask you first if it was okay. And Miss Wills, she said if I called her that again she was going to cook for me. Mr. Stone told me that I'd better stop because having Willow cook for a person was paramount to having a death sentence."

Alex laughed again and pulled him to him for a hug. "You go ahead and call them grand whatever and just for me once can you call Wills Miss Wills while I'm around. I'll make sure that Jared, Uncle Jared to you, does all your cooking when you go to his house. But I want to see her face when you do it."

"You're very strange, Mr. Alex. Very." Alex started to ask him to drop the "Mr." Part, but Jack beat him to it. "I guess I could call you Dad, couldn't I? I mean, if you don't mind."

Alex felt his heart melt and tears well in his eyes. "No, son. I won't mind that one bit. In fact, it would make me very proud."

# Chapter 23

Everything was in place. Everyone who needed to be here was here. Jack was at school, Grandda was going to work, and Alex was in his office. The police and the FBI agents were spread all over the house pretending to be workmen. Mr. Stone…Jared was making sure they didn't take down a wall in their enthusiasm.

Heather wished she was at work too. But Alex had said that he wanted her close. Plus, no one wanted the trouble taken to the bakery if at all possible. So she was cooking here, trying to relieve the stress, making cookies and bread to fill the time.

At nine o'clock, she was up to her elbows in bread dough when Candace came into the kitchen. She made Heather nervous. She wasn't entirely sure why, she just did.

"Mmmm, homemade bread. Is that for here?" Heather nodded at her question. "I love warm bread fresh from the oven. Especially when I don't have to make it. Jared is a good cook. Did you know that?"

"Yes, ma'am. He made me breakfast this morning. The lady who owns the bakery where I work, Miss

217

Caroline, she and her daughter sometimes have an entire loaf for lunch between them. They just slice it up as soon as I take it out of the oven."

"Oh that sounds so delicious. Maybe you and I can have one like that, you think? We could invite Willow, but she was called away to the site early this morning. Frankly, I think Alex is happy. He didn't want her here just in case." Candace leaned close to Heather and whispered, "She's a bit blood thirsty when she thinks someone is going to be hurt."

Heather had heard her leave. Jared had been banging around in the kitchen when she had come downstairs before seeing Jack off to school. She didn't know what to think when he'd made her sit down and he fixed her breakfast. He hadn't said a single word other than, "sit," which she had. The omelet was the best she'd ever eaten and before she could tell him so, he stomped off in the direction of the living room and had not come back.

"Actually, Heather, I'm glad we're alone. I wanted to ask you a few things." Heather's belly churned when Candace pulled out a notepad and a pen. "I have a list for everything. I think that's where Willow gets it from."

"Maybe you should ask Alex. He knows...I told him everything. I don't know why my mother attacked him. She doesn't even like me so why she thought...maybe she was protecting him. She thinks I'm a whore anyway. Then there...then there—I'm going to be sick."

Heather took off for the little half bath on the first floor. She'd just managed to get the door shut when she started throwing up. The knock at the door had her groaning. She didn't want anyone to hear her.

"Heather, honey, are you all right?" Alex. What was he doing? Candace had probably gotten him. "Heather?"

"Please, I'm fine. Just nerves, that's all." The door opened behind her and she heard him walk in. "I'm all right. I was just nervous. I think your mom wants you. Would you go make—"

"Hush. Here, take this please." He handed her a wet cloth and she wiped her mouth with it. "Can you stand up yet?"

"I don't know. Why don't you go to your mom? I'm fine, really. I just want to sit here a moment." She leaned back against the wall and closed her eyes. "I'm just going to close my eyes for a minute."

She was surprised when he sat beside her. "You scared her, my mom. She came running in my office and said you were sick. All sorts of things ran through my head when she said that. You've no idea how scared I was."

"I'm so sorry. I'm all right now. I was just...I don't handle stress well. I throw up when things get stressful. I can do all right in a crisis when someone needs me, but I fall apart after it's over. I guess it's been a bit much over the past few days."

He chuckled. "Yeah, I would say so. Are you better now? You look it." She nodded at him. "I think there's a toothbrush in that drawer there. I keep a new one down here in case the bathroom upstairs is under construction."

She pulled it out and the little sample-sized tube of toothpaste. She was using it when he stood up behind her and put his arms around her waist. It wasn't sexual; at least it didn't feel that way, more comforting than anything.

"Heather," he asked softly. "Why were you nervous? Mom wouldn't hurt you or say anything to you to upset you. She can be very ferocious when need be, but she loves with all her heart."

She wrapped her hands over his arms. It felt good. Not unlike when Jack held her but more sensual. She rinsed her mouth and leaned back against him. Without turning around, she answered him. "I thought she was going to ask me about why my mom hit you. Or maybe, I don't know, what I was doing with you." She turned in his arms then and looked up at him. "Why am I with you Alex? I don't understand that myself."

"Because I love you. With all my heart." He kissed her on the mouth quickly then the nose. "She said you were making bread. Can I get some with my lunch, you think?"

"Your mom wants a loaf for lunch." Heather pulled away. "I'll go and tell her I'm sorry. I don't know enough about families to know how to react to one. I'm sorry."

"You should tell her that," he said as they came out of the bathroom. "She'll understand. She was afraid she'd made you mad at her. She likes you a lot."

Heather nodded and walked down the hall. She had messed up again. She decided when she got to the kitchen, she was going to put on a happy face if it killed her. Heather walked into the kitchen and stopped dead in her tracks. Alex bumped into her. She knew the exact moment when he realized what she'd seen.

"Hello, Alexander. So nice of you to join us. I was just telling your mommy here that you've been a bad boy. I've been waiting for you for days." The man holding a gun to Candace's head looked crazy and worst yet, he knew Alex. "Why don't you and your pretty maid come in and have a seat? We're going to have a nice talk. Starting with whatever it is your dead ex-partner told you before he was supposed to be dead."

~~~

Alex's heart stopped beating for several seconds then it began to pump like a jackhammer. Mik had a gun pointed at his mom.

"Let her go and I'll do whatever it is you want. Just let her go, please." Alex raised his hands up as he moved in front of Heather. "I swear I'll do whatever it is you want if you just let go of my mom."

"Oh, I know you'll do what I want." Mik nodded to the chairs and he and Heather sat down. "You should have stayed with the company when I came to you. There was no reason whatsoever to be all high and mighty and leave like you didn't trust me."

"Looks to me like he had good reason to." The gun popped his mom on the head when she spoke.

Alex started to rise, but the gun was suddenly back at her head. "Don't hurt her. I swear to Christ if you hurt her again, you'll have to kill me," Alex said through clenched teeth. "Let her go."

"You're in no position to bargain with me or give me demands, Alexander. You'll do what I want and maybe I'll let her live. But you...you're not." Mik nodded at Heather. "You, girl, fix some coffee for everyone. And don't do anything stupid or your next check could be covered in blood."

When Heather stood up, he could see her trembling. He wanted to protect her and keep her and his mom safe. He'd done this, brought this to them. He should have made them leave yesterday, or not come at all when they'd made this plan.

When Jack had explained to him what he'd found, Alex's dad had called a friend of his at the Bureau. Within an hour, Jack was explaining again what he'd found.

"The remote access is only for this computer." He pointed to the IP address in the corner of the computer. "It can command and take over the other computer it's attached to right now and unless someone moves the cursor, the other person won't know it's happening."

"What have you found on the other computer? How much hacking have you done? Tell me now, kid, and I'll go easier on you." Heather started forward then, a mamma bear protecting her cub, when Alex's dad stepped in.

"I'll have you know my grandson wouldn't do such a thing. He told me immediately what he'd discovered and if that's attitude you have, then you can get the hell out of my house."

"Edgar." Tomas Gomez patted his long time friend on the back. "Not everyone knows you the way I do. I'm sorry, son. Tell us what you know, or figured out. This man"—he glared at the man who had made the accusation—"will keep his mouth shut or he'll answer to me."

"There are accounts too. Would you like to see them?" Alex leaned closer to the computer and watched as Jack pulled up the ten accounts that Brick had told him about. "There is another one too, but the password is protected. I'm seeing if I can get the computer to find his password to it."

"But you know how to get it, don't you?" Alex asked with a grin. "You either know how to get it or you're working on it."

Jack flushed. "It was a program that I found that can help you find a password if you don't know one. You know, make one up. I thought I could use it in reverse. Sort of make it figure one out with the right query. All the information is on the other computer. The program will play with all the other passwords he has saved and see what it can extrapolate."

"So let me get this straight," Tomas asked Jack as he sat down. "You are using a program to help say me find a password to figure out a password? And what do you mean saved passwords? You mean like when it says do you want the computer to remember this one?"

"Yes, sir. You should never let it remember your password. It's too easy to hack into them and get them. People lose identities that way and some people who save their credit card information on a site they buy from? The hacker can use that information to make all sorts of purchases that you don't know about and change your password so you can't get in and stop it until it's too late."

"So this program is going in and finding his saved passwords and is now going to use them against him." Jack was already shaking his head and Alex simply smiled. "What do you mean no? You just told me that's what you're doing."

"He said he's hoping it will find it. It sounds like it will work in theory. But if he doesn't have the words saved, that could be one problem. Or if it's too complicated, it could take days to work, if it even does." Alex winked at Jack. "Not bad for a ten-year-old, huh?"

"I'm only nine. I won't be ten until February fourteenth." Jack flushed again. "Mom said I would forever be her sweetheart. Mushy girl stuff."

Alex was brought back to the present by a cuff to the head. The pain exploded in his head like he'd been shot. He looked up at Mik and felt the blood seep down his cheek. He glared at the man and refused to wipe it off.

"I said come with me. And when I have you in the car with me, I'll let your mommy go. Now get up." Mik started moving toward the door with his mom.

Alex could see the Feds outside. "I don't think so. You won't be going anywhere. Why don't you let my mom go and the officers outside will take you without hurting you. I swear it." Alex stood and he could hear Heather whimper. "You'll have safe passage to jail and nobody has to get hurt."

Mik looked panicky for the first time. He held the gun tighter to his mom's head and glared. Heather stepped forward and stopped, her eyes going wide.

"No, don't. Don't do it, please." She started forward again and Mik pointed the gun at her. Alex stopped.

"You let my grandma go, mister. I'm going to shoot you if you don't." Alex looked in the door way to see Jack standing there with a nail gun. His entire world went tunnel vision.

"What the fuck are you gonna do, kid, shoot me? I don't think so. Not with that little thing." Mik held Alex's mom tighter to him. "You need to get your ass over here with the rest of the family. Alex, make your son list—"

"I said to let my grandma go. I just got her and I don't want anything to happen to her. And this gun can shoot one hundred pounds per square inch in less than a tenth of a second. How thick do you think your head is?"

Alex might have thought it was funny if the situation wasn't so grave. The framing nailer looked so huge in Jack's hand. Alex could see the police and other personnel behind him just out of sight. Alex wanted one of them to step up and grab his son and pull him out of the way. But he could see they were moving in position to do that.

"Jack, put the gun down, son, and walk away. He'll shoot you if he gets the chance. Please, honey, move back." Heather was walking toward her son and right in front of Mik.

"Heather, don't—"

"Fuck this shit. You're all going to die." Mik pressed the gun to his mom's head and said, "Say good night Gracie," and then stiffened.

His body jerked a second then a third time before he dropped the gun and staggered back, taking his mom with him. As Alex leapt forward to grab her, Heather pulled her away and the police opened fire.

# Chapter 24

The police and the Feds poured in the house. Jack was scooped up by Jared and pulled out of the way. Alex grabbed his mom's hand and held it while someone was talking. Finally, he had his chin jerked around and he looked at Heather. He couldn't quite focus on what she was saying, but he could see her mouth moving. He was pushed to the floor and flat on his back when things started to come to him.

Sounds at first. There was someone shouting. Then he could hear sirens. Alex looked over at Heather who was still talking to him and he could hear her, but not well. He tried to concentrate and finally, with his head swimming, he could understand some of it. But not enough to know what was going on.

"…okay. She's going to be okay. I gave her an ice pack and the medic is looking at her now. Please, you're scaring me, Alex. Talk to me. Tell me you're going to be okay. Please? I love you. Please don't die on me."

"Jack?" He knew something about Jack, something had happened. There had been gunshots, he remembered now. "Where is he? He okay too?"

"Mr. Stone took him to the office. He shot him with that big thingy. He actually…I'm going to ground him but good for skipping school. He should have been at school."

Alex tried to smile at her anger, but couldn't quite manage it. "Jared. Not Mr. Stone. Jared. Why did Jack shoot Jared?" Alex tried to raise his head. "Hurts. Fuzzy. Mom? Is mom—"

"She's fine, the medic said. She has a nasty bump on her head, but she's going to be fine. Your dad is with her now. Not Jared, the man holding the gun on us. Are you hurting? He shot you, you big dummy." She smacked his arm. "They're going to take you both to the hospital."

Alex faded out for a while, he knew, because the next time he opened his eyes, he was strapped to a gurney and Heather was holding his hand crying. He squeezed it and she looked at him.

"I don't think this is going to be a good start to our marriage if this is the way things are going to go. I can't take this kind of pressure." He smiled at her. "I usually lead a very sedate life. Will you have sex with me when I get home? I need you." Alex heard someone laugh, but couldn't stay awake any longer.

When he woke again, he was in a bed, stationary this time. He looked around the room and realized he was in the hospital. When he tried to sit up, someone pushed him back down with a firm hand.

"Stay there or they'll try to tie you down again. I don't know if they'll survive your wife tearing into them again." A soft chuckle then, "She's got quite a temper on her, your wife."

"Dad?" It hurt to try and see. "What happened? I know that Mik was there and—Mom, is mom all right? He had a gun pointed at her head."

"She's fine. She took Heather down to the cafeteria to get something to eat. Wills went with them. Jared has Jack at his house." A light, very dim, came on as his dad continued. "He's not too happy about it, but his mom told him to pick out a puppy and to make sure it was the one he wanted. He's a bright boy. Told her right off that he knew it was to keep him busy and he didn't appreciate her treating him like a baby." After a brief pause, he asked, "How you feeling, son?"

Alex tried to remember what had happened. "He said he was going to shoot him if he didn't let his new grandma go. Jack had a nailer. I remember thinking it looked so big in his hand."

His dad nodded. "Tomas said that he shot Mik three times with it. Twice in the back, the third in the head. The pressure wasn't very high or he might have killed him. As it was, the two officers that were still awake did it."

"Awake? I don't understand. Why were they awake and how did Mik get past them?" Alex was starting to remember things more clearly now. He'd been shot. He looked down at his belly then away quickly. "They didn't come. I thought they'd be all over the place when he showed up."

"He was in the house. He was already in the house by the time the agents and everyone showed up. He probably didn't know they were agents, but he did drug everyone. Something in the water they used in the coffee maker. Lucky for us, Jared stopped drinking coffee when Wills got pregnant. He was able to roust a few of them and get them to the kitchen." Edgar reached out and took his hand. "Your wife. She is something else. When your mom was laying there on the floor, Heather sounded like a drill sergeant getting people in place and getting the medics there. When your mom said she could get up and help, Heather tore into her like a mother protecting her cub. Candace laid back down right quick after that. You, however, she begged you to wake up. I think at one point she might have ordered you to get up."

Alex smiled as he closed his eyes. He'd thought the same thing about her and Jack and how protective they were of each other. "She is something else. I love her very much."

His dad cleared his throat. "You might want to tell her that a lot when she comes back. She's a mite mad at you."

"Me?" he shouted, and then immediately lowered his voice when it felt like a knife was going through his head. "What the hell did I do? I'm shot, did she notice that?" He looked at his dad's smile. "Oh, God, what did I do?"

"Yeah, well, she seems to be mad about you telling the medic you wanted her to...well, you made some comments about...son, you'd better ask her. She was pretty pissed off when she—"

The door opened and the three women walked in. Alex could only see Heather. She looked beautiful to him. She had tears in her eyes when she took his other hand and kissed it.

"It's all right, honey. I'm fine. Head hurts a bit and I'm sure I have some pain in my gut. I guess there's no real damage."

"No real damage. No real...do you have any idea what I've gone through because you have no real damage? You hard-headed, chauvinistic, pompous ass. You told that man you'd go with him. Go with him and leave me alone. He would have killed you." Alex noticed that his family left the room and he thought they were all traitors. "Then you tell the ambulance driver and the medic, and oh let's not forget the nurses that were taking care of you, that I was the best lay you'd ever had, that I was the most, and I quote, 'wonderfulest wife you've ever known.' And if that wasn't enough, you—"

He pulled her down and kissed her. Her mouth was hard at first, but he pulled her down across him and she wrapped herself around him, careful of his wounds. He shifted her slightly and fit her in his arms even as his head pounded. When he finally lifted his head, he looked down into her teary face. "I'm so sorry that I scared you. But I couldn't let him take you, or my mom. I didn't want to lose either one of you." He held her when she tried to get up. "No, I need to hold you. Please, baby, just let me hold you."

Neither of them said anything for several minutes. Then she started talking softly. "Jack killed that man. I know they said he didn't, but I saw those nails go into him. He said he's all right with it because he was able to save us, but I don't know."

"He'll be fine. He's a brilliant little boy." Alex decided if he wasn't okay later, he'd get him the best care in the world. Alex owed him a great deal.

"Your dad, he was so mad at those men for leaving us there without help. I thought he was going to have a heart attack. Then when he found out they'd been drugged, he was so sorry. He's…my mom wouldn't have cared. But he did. He apologized to each and every one of them."

"Dad always told Wills and me that if you're wrong, nothing will make you a bigger person than admitting it and telling the person you messed up. I've tried to live by that, and I think Wills does too." He closed his eyes again and simply held her. He loved her and she did him. He was going to have to hear her say it again without tears in her eyes, he decided.

~~~

Jack sat quietly and watched his new dad sleep. The nurse had told Jack to wake him, but he just wanted to watch. Jack was actually sort of nervous. He knew he'd messed up by skipping school and didn't want Alex to yell at him.

He startled when Alex said his name. Jack started crying, not because he'd scared him, but because he didn't want to disappoint Alex. He hated crying, but just couldn't seem to stop. He wanted to be adopted so badly.

"I'm really sorry, sir. I couldn't leave her all alone. She won't tell me when she's hurt or tired, and she and Grandpa Tom are all I got. Well, I have Vickie, but I don't count her. But he was a bad man, really bad man. They found those two dead men at that house. Mom doesn't know I know about them, but I can read. I used your computer and I didn't ask, I know, but gran…Mr. James said I could. Then there was—"

"Jack!" Jack shut up when Alex shouted his name. "Take a deep breath, buddy. Now, slow down. Let's start from the top, okay?" Jack nodded. "I'm proud of you."

"You are?" Jack looked behind him to see if Alex might have been talking to someone else. "For real?"

His mom was always saying that to him, and his grandpa Tom. He'd had a teacher tell him once, but he didn't think the man was very nice about it. Something about his tone had put Jack's dander up, as his grandpa Tom called it.

Alex laughed. "Yes, for real. You saved your grandma. And probably the rest of the house."

"You're not mad because I skipped school? Mom sure is. She said I'm grounded until I'm fifty. I thought that was a long time for just skipping school, but she had her foot going and I thought it best to shut up."

"You're probably safer that way. Tell me, are you going to skip school ever again?"

Jack wanted to say no, never, but didn't want to lie. Something may happen and he might have to. He looked at the man who he already loved more than he thought possible right in the eye. "Are you going to have stupid people come to your home and try to murder us all?" Jack could have bitten his tongue off and wished he could take it all back. But Alex laughed.

"Good point. I'll try not to invite mass murders to the house again and you try not to skip school. Deal?" Alex put out his hand and Jack took it, feeling very grown up. "Okay, you mentioned your grandda letting you use my computer. By the way, he's your grandda just like I'm your dad. Computer usage...computer usage... I'm not sure about that one."

Jack felt the disappointment throughout his whole body. He'd been having so much fun using the small laptop in Ale...Dad's office. It was much faster and nicer than the ones they had at school.

"You don't get on any sites that would make your mom mad at me, do you? I mean like...you know...porn sites?"

Jack felt the flush heat his face he was so embarrassed. "No! Mom would skin me alive if I did that. And ewww. Naked people? No thanks. Gross. It's bad enough when you kiss my mom." Jack shuddered. "Gross."

"Okay, kid, I get it." Alex laughed again. "The computer is fine. Use it when you want. Maybe we'll see about getting one for your room. Smart as you are on mine, I may just have you as my partner in business. We'll be James and Son Computers someday."

Jack felt so much pride in that simple statement he couldn't stop from getting up and kissing Dad on the cheek. When he hugged him back, Jack felt the tears threaten to spill, but this time, he didn't care or feel embarrassed by them.

"Jack, there's one more thing I wanted to tell you. You don't only just have your mom and grandpa Tom anymore. You have me, my parents, who I think might already be getting you too much for Christmas, an aunt and uncle and all my relatives as well. You'll have so many people pinching your cheek at Christmas you might change your mind about me adopting you."

"I'll never do that. Never." Jack sat back in the chair, suddenly exhausted. He'd not had a very good night the past few nights worrying about Dad and whether or not he'd change his mind.

Dad. Jack liked the sound of that. He never thought his mom would marry. She'd never even dated as far as he knew. She had friends, he supposed, but nobody who made her light up the way Dad did.

Jack was excited about his first real Christmas with a family and no matter what Dad said, he was looking forward to having family. He'd gladly have his cheeks pinched for a chance to be around a lot of people. Jack felt his body relax and thought he'd just close his eyes a minute before he called his grandda to come and get him.

Jack was thinking about having a brother or sister too as his mind grew fuzzy and his body more lax. Someone he could be the big brother to. He tried to open his eyes when he heard someone come in the room, but when Dad laughed, Jack let his body go. Yes, he thought drifting into sleep, having a family was going to be so much fun.

## Before You Go...

# HELP AN AUTHOR

## *write a review*

# THANK YOU!

Share your voice and help guide other readers to these wonderful books. Even if it's only a line or two your reviews help readers discover the author's books so they can continue creating stories that you'll love. Login to your favorite retailer and leave a review. Thank you.

AWARD WINNING, BESTSELLING AUTHOR

Kathi Barton, author of the bestselling series Force of Nature, lives in Nashport, Ohio with her husband Paul. In addition to writing full time Kathi likes to spend time with her eight grandkids, three children and three children-in-laws. She writes to relax and have fun.

Her muse, a cross between Jimmy Stewart and Hugh Jackman brings them to life for her readers in a way that has them coming back time and again for more. Her favorite genre is paranormal romance with a great deal of spice. You can visit Kathi on line and drop her an email if you'd like. She loves hearing from her fans. aaronskiss@gmail.com.

Follow Kathi on her blog:
http://kathisbartonauthor.blogspot.com/

www.ingramcontent.com/pod-product-compliance
Lightning Source LLC
Chambersburg PA
CBHW032211190626
46810CB00019B/2657